Th
wa

A
turned upsi..
resolutions and betrayed her parents' trust. Now ..
has an agonizing decision to make which will affect all
their lives. Amid all the turmoil and heartbreak, there is
only one person who seems to understand what Cass is
going through—the last person in the world that Cass
would have chosen as a friend, the yobbish bully, James
Derwent.

But James has problems of his own, and when these
reach a crisis can Cass help him as he had helped her?
And will she be in time . . . ?

SUE WELFORD was born in Sussex and trained to be a secretary
before giving up paid work to bring up her children. When they
started school, she had several part-time jobs, and then became
an editorial writer with a local newspaper. When she was made
redundant, she continued writing at home and had several articles
published in magazines. After five rejected novels, her first book
for young adults was published in 1989. *Nowhere to Run* is the
eighth of her books to be published by Oxford University Press.

Nowhere to Run

Other books by Sue Welford

The Night After Tomorrow
Starlight City
The Shadow of August
Turning Point
Out of the Blue

Nowhere to Run

Sue Welford

OXFORD
UNIVERSITY PRESS

OXFORD
UNIVERSITY PRESS

Great Clarendon Street, Oxford OX2 6DP

Oxford University Press is a department of the University of Oxford.
It furthers the University's objective of excellence in research, scholarship,
and education by publishing worldwide in

Oxford New York

Athens Auckland Bangkok Bogotá Buenos Aires Calcutta
Cape Town Chennai Dar es Salaam Delhi Florence Hong Kong Istanbul
Karachi Kuala Lumpur Madrid Melbourne Mexico City Mumbai
Nairobi Paris São Paulo Shanghai Singapore Taipei Tokyo Toronto Warsaw

and associated companies in Berlin Ibadan

Oxford is a registered trade mark of Oxford University Press
in the UK and in certain other countries

British Library Cataloguing in Publication Data available

ISBN 0 19 275140 9

1 3 5 7 9 10 8 6 4 2

Typeset by AFS Image Setters Ltd, Glasgow

Printed in Great Britain by
Cox & Wyman Ltd, Reading, Berkshire

Sun shimmers on water. Trees quiver in the breeze. Shadows dance on the grass. People walk. Prams, wheels squeaking, bump over kerbs. Kids run, yell, trip, cry . . . all these things a blur, like suddenly squinting into light.

Beside me, James is stretched out on the grass, face up to the sun, asleep . . . or pretending.

This moment . . . the sun, the water, James . . . everyone. I decide to write it all down in case, one day, we forget.

PART ONE

PART ONE

1

I knew I'd been stupid. I didn't need Mel to tell me.

When I first told her what I'd done I giggled and laughed like a silly little kid. I just couldn't help it. It was the most momentous, scary thing I'd ever done in my life. I suppose the enormity of it hadn't quite hit me yet.

'You didn't!' Mel squealed, thinking I was having her on. 'Oh, Cass!'

'I did,' I said. 'Honestly. Don't you think he was just the best-looking guy in the room, though.'

'Well . . . not exactly.' Mel had sobered up by now. 'I mean he was cool, but more your type than mine. Long hair and baggy T-shirts and that kind of stuff are not really my scene.'

She was right. The boy I'd met at Emma's party, Steve, was just the type of boy I dreamed about. Laid back, relaxed, easy blue eyes that stare at you and seem to be trying to read your mind. Mel likes boys with short hair and smart clothes, in fact her regular boyfriend, Michael, looks like something out of a fashion mag. Not my cup of tea at all.

It had all started when Emma's parents went away for the weekend and she decided it was a great chance to have a party. She'd invited everyone in our class, me included.

'Come on, Cass,' Mel had said in one of her wheedling kind of voices as we strolled down the school corridor during lunch break. 'It'll do you good to let your hair down. You can't spend your whole life stuck in your room, dreaming.'

5

'I don't spend my whole life dreaming,' I protested although I knew what she said was true. Well, almost true anyway. I did do *some* other things besides school work and reading and listening to my CDs and, I suppose I *had* to admit it, dreaming about all the things I wanted to do with my life. I liked swimming and walking in the park and going to the movies and watching TV and stuff. I certainly didn't like parties much though. And I didn't go round with a crowd like most other people. I guess being an only child makes you happy with your own company.

My only real friend is Mel. Tall, willowy, dark hair cut short and spiky. Eyes that are quick and darting, she's full of the self-confidence you'd die for. As friends I suppose we balance one another out. I'm quieter, more thoughtful than her. I'm also fairly short with long, straight sort of reddish mousy hair and brown eyes and hateful snub nose with freckles on. I suppose I calm Mel down, make her stop and think about things a bit. And she livens me up. Persuades me to go swimming when I'm in the middle of reading a great book, or drags me off to see the latest Disney movie when I'd much rather wait for something more serious. And that's why she was trying to persuade me to go to Emma's party. I hadn't been out anywhere for ages and she'd decided it was about time I did.

I was racking my brains for an excuse *not* to go. I'd gone from inventing a visit from a distant relative to needing to finish an essay. I'd just decided to tell her the truth and say I simply didn't fancy it when a crowd of boys from our class came charging in through the double doors. They almost knocked me and Mel for six.

'For God's sake, you maniacs!' She made a dive for her bag that had gone spinning across the corridor.

I'd been luckier, dodging out of the way before one of them, fat slob Derwent, hurtled into me. As it was, he just gave me a gorilla grin and said 'Sorry, Cass . . . I *don't* think,' then burst out laughing and went off with the others, sniggering and making snide remarks over their shoulders. Fatty Derwent and his mates were pigs. They were always in trouble, getting hauled up to the Head for some act of vandalism or other.

Before Mel could get her bag, another of the animals, Nick Mallon, began using it as a football, kicking it along the corridor in front of him while the others cheered. Stuff spilled out. Her Jackie Collins paperback, make-up bag, hairbrush and, horror of horrors, a packet of Tampax. Red with rage she shot off after Nick and grabbed his jacket, pulling him away. He laughed again as she scooped up her things. She came back, still seething, her bag clutched to her chest.

'God, I hate those animals!' She stuffed everything back in.

'Me too.' I think I would have died if a packet of *my* tampons had fallen out in front of those guys. But Mel didn't seem particularly bothered now they'd gone. She was always quick to flare up but never stayed mad for long. She linked her arm through mine, forgetting about the boys and carrying on trying to persuade me to go to Emma's party.

'*Please* come, Cass,' she said. 'It'll be great, I know it will.'

And I couldn't come up with an excuse quick enough, so I said yes.

Later, when I told my mum, she seemed pleased.

'You really do spend too much time in your room, Cass,' she said. 'I know you've got a lot of studying to do and it's great you're getting on so well at school but you've got to have *some* fun.'

I sighed. 'Yeah, I suppose so.' I was perched on the kitchen stool while she peeled the spuds for the evening meal. I hadn't told her Emma's parents were going away. And, strangely, she didn't ask. Maybe she'd just taken it for granted that they would be at home. I wondered afterwards, when the damage was done, if she'd have been so keen for me to go if she'd known they weren't going to be there.

'I'll come and pick you up,' she said. 'Midnight, OK?'

I grinned. 'Is that when my dress turns to rags?'

She turned from the sink, grinning back. 'That'll be the day,' she said.

'What?' I said. 'My dress turning to rags?'

She laughed. 'No . . . when you wear a dress instead of those tatty old jeans.'

'You know, to be honest, I was pretty surprised to see you slink off with Steve,' Mel said the morning after the party.

'I didn't *slink* off,' I protested.

'Well . . . you know what I mean,' she said. 'You'd only just met him. Don't you think it was a bit risky?'

I shrugged. I knew she was right. 'Yeah,' I said with another sigh. 'I guess it was.'

I was sitting on the bottom stair, talking to her on the phone. I'd got a terrible headache. A hangover, I suppose. I'd caught sight of myself as I stumbled down to pick up the receiver. I looked as if I'd got the starring role in a horror movie. Hair sticking up like straw, pale skin, eyes bleary with lack of sleep. My mouth felt like the bottom of the parrot's cage and I ached all over. People say you forget what happens when you've had too much to drink. It's a lie. You don't. At least, I didn't. I remembered it all. Before, during . . . and after.

Steve was a friend of Emma's brother, visiting them from California. He was taking a year out to travel round Europe before going to college. Blond hair, tanned skin. I could hardly take my eyes off him. We'd danced so close you couldn't have got a pin between us. And when he whispered in my ear, I'd staggered upstairs without a second thought. I couldn't help myself. I wasn't able to say no. I didn't want to say a single word. I only wanted to drown in the glow of his eyes, the feel of his hands, the smell of his aftershave. The way he groaned into my hair.

'Oh, Cass . . . Cass . . . Cass . . . ' My whole body went soft as if I was made of cotton wool.

Mel wasn't the only one who was surprised I'd gone upstairs with Steve. I was too. Me, Cass Andrews, who was saving herself for someone she had been going out with for ages and ages and who she really loved. Cass, whose first experience of sex was going to be the most romantic and beautiful thing ever. The thing I hadn't bargained for was being so knocked out Steve had even asked me I hadn't even thought of saying no.

I hadn't kept count of how many drinks I'd had. You don't after the first two or three. Especially those alcopops, so yummy you don't realize how drunk you're getting. How stupid you're starting to behave, as if someone else had invaded your body and taken over. How reality is getting further and further away and you haven't even noticed.

But it hadn't only been the booze . . . it had been everything. The music, the heat, couples twined round one another. Nothing in the world could have stopped me.

'Did he use anything?' Mel's question brought me back to earth with a crash.

My stomach turned over. It was something I'd avoided thinking about. Locking it away in that corner of my mind I keep for things I want to forget.

'I'm not sure,' I admitted.

'Cass . . . you're joking!' I knew she was horrified.

'It was all so quick . . . and dark,' I said pathetically.

My heart lurched when I thought about it. The way we had locked the door then sunk down on the pile of coats on Emma's parents' bed. Already glued together as if nothing could prise us apart.

Giggling, laughing, sighing, groaning.

Boring old me. He wanted *me*. No one like him had ever fancied me before. Boys I did like generally fancied

9

someone else. Because I didn't hang out with a crowd they thought I was stuck up and didn't bother about me. It's not true. I'm *not* stuck up. It's just the way I am.

I'd been sitting on the floor watching everyone else enjoying themselves when Steve had come in from the kitchen and sat down beside me. He started talking to me as if I was the most attractive girl in the room.

'You have got something, haven't you?' I'd mumbled later when it all turned deadly serious and it was far too late to turn back. Even if I'd wanted to.

He told me he had and I believed him. I was dizzy, drunk not only on alcopop but on him. His mouth, his hands, his skin, his urgency . . . dizzy, dizzy, dizzy. Being with him sent me soft and spinning into a tornado of feelings I didn't know I'd got.

Only afterwards I wasn't *really* sure whether he'd used a condom or not.

Mel had lapsed into silence. She was obviously gobsmacked. Speechless with my stupidity. I could almost read her thoughts. She couldn't even bear to put them into words. Surely not me . . . how could sensible old me have been that silly? My thoughts were like frantic fishes swimming in the whirlpool of my mind. Maybe I'd wake up in a minute and find it was all some terrible drowning dream.

'Well, don't worry, Cass,' Mel said in a softer voice, sorry she'd been critical. 'It'll probably be all right.'

But she was wrong.

It wasn't.

2

'She's *what*?'

I could hear my dad's shout even from where I was lying. On my bed, petrified, eyes screwed up. Escaping. Hoping the world would go away. Wishing I was in another place, another time, wanting the nightmare to be over.

This isn't happening, I was thinking . . . this really isn't happening. I opened my eyes and stared at my dolphin poster on the wall. Blue sea and sky, the creature a shining arc coming out of the waves. How I wished I could be swimming in the ocean with it. By my window I'd hung the dreamcatcher my gran brought me back when she went to Texas. It's a white one, white circle above soft, twirling white feathers. She told me that according to Native American tradition, a mother would weave a dreamcatcher to hang above her baby's cradle. Only good dreams would be able to pass through, the bad ones would get tangled up and when the sun rose and touched it, the nightmares would dissolve. I used to believe it worked but now I knew different.

'Let *me* tell your dad,' Mum said a month after the party when I'd at last plucked up the courage to tell her and she'd stopped crying and raving on at me.

I'd already done one test but she insisted on doing another. That was positive too. Not that I'd really needed to do even one. My period was two weeks late. When I got out of bed in the mornings I felt like throwing up, my boobs felt as if they were on fire and I

11

felt totally awful all over. I didn't need a degree in biology to know what was happening to me.

For a week I'd done everything I could to make my period start. Aerobics every day, working out in the gym, jumping up and down, running everywhere, galloping up and down the stairs. It hadn't worked. Nothing had. Finally I'd got no choice. I *had* to tell my mum.

'Why didn't you tell me straight away, Cassandra?' she had yelled angrily. That was the first bad sign. No one ever called me that unless they were furious with me. 'We could at least have got you the morning-after pill.'

But how *could* I have told her? How could I admit I'd been so brainless. She'd have gone absolutely ballistic.

And now . . . too late . . . crying wouldn't do any good. Nothing would. But I just couldn't help it.

'Does Dad have to know?' I sobbed when Mum said she'd be the one to tell him.

I was being hopeless . . . a wimp. Still sore from the way she'd shouted at me when all I'd wanted was for her to put her arms around me and tell me everything was going to be all right.

Mum looked at me and for a minute hope blazed. Maybe Dad didn't have to know how badly I'd let him down?

But . . .

'We're a family,' she said. 'We should share our troubles. Don't worry, I'll pick a good moment.'

But there wasn't a good moment to tell a man his beloved sixteen-year-old daughter was pregnant. The daughter he'd always been so proud of. The one he and Mum had cherished and protected, taking her wherever she wanted to go, doing whatever she wanted to do. Pony riding, camping, up in a glider when she was seven because she had wanted to know what it felt like to be a bird. The one Dad spoiled and called his little pippin because he had said she was the apple of his eye, whatever that meant. The one he hoped would fulfil *his* dreams, grasp hold of all the opportunities he'd never had.

'*You can do anything you want with a brain like yours, Cass,*' he said. '*University, a great career . . . the world's your oyster.*'

He'd told me that ever since I could remember. So often I thought how disappointed he'd be if I didn't come up to his expectations.

Well, it looked as if I was just about to find out.

I'd spent the first weeks after the party hoping, worrying, waiting. Waiting for Steve to ring, for one thing. Then, desperately ringing Emma's house to find out if he was there. I wanted to see him, talk to him. The dizzy memory of that night just wouldn't go away. It was still sitting in my brain like a beautiful painting or film you thought would be lodged there for ever. Only now, a month later, I could see it hadn't been beautiful at all. It had just been frantic, sordid groping that didn't mean a single thing. I still could hardly believe I'd actually done it. Abandoned all the promises I'd made myself. Amongst other things . . . like vowing to be sensible for the rest of my life and desperately seeking ways I could make it up to my mum, I'd vowed one definite thing. I'd never, ever get drunk again. And that was a promise I really knew I would keep.

But when I phoned Emma I discovered Steve had gone. Back to the States without even calling me. I'd just been a name urgently whispered in the dark.

I was silly not to have phoned before but I'd been too proud. Not too proud to stay in hoping he would ring, though. Or too proud to walk past Emma's house on every possible occasion in case he came out and just happened to bump into me. Just too proud to let him know I cared.

'Don't be so hard on yourself,' Mel had said. 'Everyone makes mistakes.'

True. But some people make bigger ones than others.

'Did he say anything about me?' I asked Emma when I phoned.

'No, he didn't actually,' she said lightly as if she wasn't giving me the worst news she possibly could. 'Why?'

Misery crashed in on me and I could hardly even answer her.

'Oh,' I mumbled. 'Nothing.'

At the other end of the phone, Emma laughed. 'Did you fancy him, then?' Then she added before I'd got the chance to say anything, 'Yes, of course you did. I remember you and him creeping off at the party. Quiet old Cass, what a surprise,' she chuckled.

My face froze. A thought flitted into my brain. Did she have any idea exactly why I was ringing? It had all been so casual. Lots of guys going off into other rooms. Everyone was too busy to notice what I was up to. It was bad enough her knowing how eager I'd been to fall into Steve's arms, let alone have me ringing up to speak to him when he'd already gone home. Some girls might have bragged about being the chosen one, considering he was so good looking and everything. Not me though. I just wanted to curl up in a corner and disappear.

'Yes, well,' I said, trying to sound light-hearted. Desperately not wanting her to know I cared. 'Even if I did, he's gone so there's no point.'

'That's true,' she said. 'Actually he saw a lot of Lynne the last week he was here so you'd be wasting your time anyway.'

Did she really mean to sound cruel?

My heart had plunged further than it already was if that was possible. Lynne! She was in our class. Noisy, blonde, big boobs, a great dancer . . . The total opposite to me. She hadn't been able to get to the party so it looked as if he'd made do with me instead.

'We're going over there at Christmas so I'll tell him you were asking about him,' Emma was saying in my ear.

14

'Don't worry about it,' I said. 'He probably won't even remember who I am.'

I slammed the phone down. How could he do that . . . ? Go off. Not remember. Not care. Not even worry in case the worst had happened. I knew I was being naive and stupid. People did that kind of stuff all the time. It looked as if being dumb was getting to be a habit.

And now sitting in my room waiting for the executioner to call, I felt worse than I had ever done in my life. I thought about all the good times we'd had as a family, holidays in Spain, Christmases with loads of presents and my dad looking daft in a red suit and cotton-wool beard. Lots of people thought you missed out if you were an only child, I knew different. It was great. And now I'd gone and spoiled everything. Everything Mum and Dad had worked for all the years of my life.

Downstairs, I heard the lounge door fly back with a crash against the wall and Dad, yelling.

'Cass! Come down here!'

I've never been frightened of my dad. Not until now. He's a great guy. A bit short on showing his emotions but then you can't have everything. He works in the city and commutes each day on the train. Mum takes him and picks him up . . . every morning, every evening for as far back as I can remember.

I suppose we're a pretty boring kind of family. Dad the breadwinner. Mum the mum. Although she's spread her wings a bit lately and enrolled in a part-time psychology course at college. Something she'd always wanted to do, she said. Strange, when all she ever seemed to want to do was be at home. At least that's what I thought. It's funny how you really think you know people then they turn out to be different altogether. Especially people so close to you as your mum.

My legs felt like jelly as I crept down the stairs. I felt so guilty I could have curled into a little ball. He'd trusted me and I'd let him down. Let myself down. And Mum. Cousins, aunts, uncles. Everyone. Dad was standing at the bottom. Waiting. His face like a hurricane.

I swallowed. My heart was beating so loudly and so fast it was like a time bomb about to go off in my chest. I suddenly saw it exploding. Bits of me splattered against the walls. Hair, skin . . . blood running down the Laura Ashley.

'Dad . . . ?'

I just stood there, hot oily tears sliding down my cheeks. I wanted him to put his arms around me like he used to when I was little. But he didn't. He just stood there stiff as a cardboard cut-out.

'Come in the sitting room,' was all he said. I couldn't blame him really. Cassandra . . . his beloved, stupid, daughter, crying because she had been dumb enough not only to have sex at sixteen but to have it with someone she didn't know and who hadn't got the good sense to use a condom, or if he had, hadn't used it properly.

He did melt a bit. Dad. At least he put his arm across my shoulders to lead me towards the sofa.

'OK, who's the father?' he demanded to know when we were all sitting down. Me staring at the blank TV screen as if there was some great movie on. Mum sitting there with a face like a tragedy.

I shrugged. 'Just some boy.'

'Some boy!' he yelled.

Mum, next to him, put her hand on his arm. 'They got carried away,' she said.

'I should think he bloody well did,' Dad raved.

'No, Dad,' I said. '*We* did. I wasn't raped or anything.'

'It's my fault,' Mum blurted out suddenly. 'I encouraged her to go to the party.'

'Don't be stupid,' I said to her. 'How can it be your fault?'

'I should have guessed what might happen,' she said.

16

'And I didn't think to ask if Emma's parents would be around.'

'You shouldn't have had to ask,' Dad said. 'Cass should have told you.'

I hung my head, not knowing what to say.

Mum was still going on. 'I know what teenage parties are like.' She shook her head. 'I should have guessed.'

'What it all boils down to,' my dad said, 'is that we trusted you, Cass.'

'I know,' I mumbled. I swallowed. 'I'm really sorry.'

Dad didn't seem to hear me. Even if he had, apologizing wouldn't have done any good. Saying you're sorry doesn't un-make things. It just makes you feel better if people know you regret what you've done. Only this time I didn't feel better at all. I just went on feeling worse and worse.

And Dad just went on ranting and raving. 'Well, who is this boy, anyway? Where does he live?'

'I don't know where he lives,' I said, scared if I told him he'd go round to Emma's and demand Steve's home address or something.

'You don't know?' Dad leaned forward. I could smell him. Stale aftershave, stale smoke from the office where he worked, beer where he'd popped in for a quickie at the pub on his way to catch the train home from work.

So I told him all I knew about Steve. Which really wasn't anything.

'Well, he'll have to pay,' Dad said. Thinking of everything in terms of money as usual.

'Look, Brian,' Mum butted in. 'It was just something that happened at a party . . . the boy lives in America . . . he won't want to know.'

Dad wiped his hand across his forehead. 'But he's responsible . . . '

'No more than I am,' I said. 'Dad, I'm not a kid any longer.'

He swallowed too. 'That's obvious,' he said. He sighed. In his day boys took the consequences if they got

17

a girl pregnant. That usually meant getting married, which was pretty silly if you hardly knew someone. 'OK, Cass, don't cry any more,' he said with a sigh. His voice softened with resignation. 'We'll sort something out.'

I sniffed and rubbed my eyes. Took the hanky he gave me to wipe away my stupidity. I looked at him, his face still swimming in front of my tears.

'No, Dad,' I said. 'It's my fault. *I'll* sort it out.'

3

But sorting out something like that isn't really something you can do yourself. Not when you're my age and you've got a secret you won't be able to hide for ever.

Mum was making all the decisions. When I really thought about it, she has always made the decisions in our family. What clothes I should wear, what school I should go to. What holidays we'd take. What new curtains we'd get or colour car, or what paint for the hall. I suppose making all the decisions had got to be such a habit she couldn't give it up.

She'd shot off down to Boots to get the second testing kit. She rang the doctor. Dad seemed to have opted out and was leaving everything to her just like he usually did. 'Do what you think's best,' he'd said wearily as if the whole thing had proved too much for him to cope with.

Best for who, I wondered?

Mum carted me off to the surgery. I didn't really want to go to our own GP. She was an old friend of Mum's and agreed to see us even though Saturday was usually reserved for emergencies. I hated the thought of her knowing.

'Can't we go to someone else?' I pleaded. 'Someone who doesn't know us?' I didn't even *want* to go to the doctor at all. I couldn't see that it was really any of her business.

'Don't be silly,' Mum said impatiently as if I was still a little girl and not a fully fledged pregnant sixteen-year-old idiot. 'She won't think anything of it. She deals with this kind of thing every day and the sooner we get things sorted, the better.'

A wave of terror crashed over me. 'What do you mean?' I said. 'Sorted?'

'Well,' Mum said. 'The operation.'

I couldn't believe it. We hadn't even discussed it. She had simply taken it for granted that's what I wanted. Although that was probably my own fault too. I might have known she'd be the one to decide what to do. And anyway, after we'd told Dad I'd run up to my room, shut myself in. Me and my misery were getting to know one another and wanted to do it in private.

But this time it was too much.

'Mum, for God's sake,' I yelled. 'You haven't even asked me!' I burst out, going red and walking round the kitchen as if I might find a path that would lead me out of all this.

Mum looked at me. 'Cass, you're such a dreamer. Sometimes I don't think you live in the real world at all.'

'What do you mean?' I blazed.

'I mean in the real world it's pretty foolish to have a baby at sixteen.'

I hung my head, my hair a shroud across my face. 'I know,' I said. 'But I'd like to have been asked what I wanted to do. For once in my life can't you let me decide something for myself?'

Her lips were a tight, white line. 'You *did* decide something for yourself and look what's happened.'

'That's a horrible thing to say,' I said even though I knew it was true.

Mum's lips were still tight. 'We'll discuss it with Janet,' she said.

'You mean *you* will,' I burst out.

She stopped drying the knives and forks and turned to face me. 'It's what you want, isn't it?' she said. 'Surely you can't actually *want* a child at your age.'

'You still could have asked,' I muttered. I looked away, swallowing the lump that was stuck in my throat. She was right, of course. It was the last thing I wanted.

She put down the tea towel and came towards me. 'I'm sorry, Cass, but you haven't been exactly talkative for the past few days, have you?'

I shook my head. She was right again. I *hadn't* been talkative. I hadn't even said much to Mel and I knew that had hurt her a lot. I couldn't help it. All I'd wanted to do was shut myself in my head and die.

And now I said a word to myself. Abortion. It sounded hateful and horrible. Almost as hateful and horrible as the thought of another person growing inside me.

Abort.

The mission is aborted.

Terminate . . . to finish . . . to end. To kill. To murder, to annihilate, to dispense with.

They were all words for exactly the same thing.

'It won't really be murder,' Mel said when she wangled out of me what was happening. 'It's not a person . . . it's just a bunch of cells . . . a zygote. Don't you remember, we did it in biology?'

I didn't remember. Zygote—I said it in my head. It was almost like a name. Zak, or Zachary . . . there was a boy in our class called that. Zebedee. Zara. Zebra. Zygote. It's supposed to be fatal to give things names—they become real then and you can't bear to part with them. But in spite of my anger with Mum for taking over my life, this was something I *could* bear to part with. In fact, I convinced myself it was something I couldn't *wait* to be rid of.

'I know it won't be murder,' I fibbed to Mel. 'And even if it was I wouldn't care.'

She had gazed at me. 'Wouldn't you?'

'No,' I'd insisted. 'Definitely not.'

So off we went to the surgery. Mum and I. Sitting speechless in the car, gazing out at the world passing by.

The great yawning gap that was growing between us was getting wider and wider with every house, every street, every tree we passed.

There hadn't really been any time to think about anything. I felt a thousand miles from nowhere. I was being tossed on the tide, drowning, and didn't seem to be able to find a way to save myself. I desperately wanted to run away and hide but I couldn't because there was nowhere to go.

'Have you thought about keeping the baby?'

Janet . . . Janet Moorhead, MD. Her name on the plaque in the surgery sounded like the title of an Australian soap. Old school mate of Mum's, white coat, Marks and Sparks polo-necked jumper, gold-rimmed specs, looked at me through her slightly tinted lenses as if I was a specimen in a jar.

Mum butted in before I could say anything.

'No.' She said it so quickly the word came out like spit. 'There's no way she can keep it.'

'Mum . . . !' I wriggled in my seat.

Doctor Janet had looked at her then back at me. 'Let Cass answer for herself,' she said.

Keep it? I hadn't let my thoughts spin that far. In fact none of it really seemed real yet and I was still hoping to wake from the nightmare. And it was obvious the thought hadn't occurred to anyone else. Otherwise why would Mum have marched me off to the surgery to get things 'sorted'?

But Mum didn't let me answer for myself as usual. A good thing this time because I seemed to have lost my power of speech.

She leaned forward. 'Look, Jan,' she said. 'She's only sixteen.' She said it as if I wasn't there which I really, really hate. 'She can't possibly know her own mind.'

Funny how parents think that just because you're young you can't possibly know what you want.

They were both looking at me now. Mum allowed me, at last, to answer for myself.

'That's not true, Mum,' I protested. 'Of course I know what I want. Being sixteen's nothing to do with it.'

'OK then,' the doc said gently. '*You* tell me, Cass.'

I swallowed and twiddled with my fingers in my lap. 'No,' I said. 'I can't keep it,' I said in a low voice. 'I don't even want it.'

'There's her exams,' Mum blurted as if Doctor Janet had demanded an explanation for my/her decision. 'Sixth form college. A child will ruin her chances of a career, won't it, Cass?'

I swallowed again. 'Yes,' I mumbled. 'Definitely.'

'What about the father?' Janet said. 'He should be consulted.'

I think it was then that Mum was really ashamed of me because for once in her life she didn't seem to be able to think of anything to say.

'No,' I murmured. 'He doesn't even know about it.'

'Don't you think you should tell him?'

I shook my head. 'Definitely not. He lives in the States . . . I didn't even really know him.' I felt mega-awful. Janet had known me since I was a baby and here I was admitting I'd had sex with a stranger. She must think I was a real waste of space. She probably even thought Mum hadn't warned me about such things. She had, though. Lots of times. Which made it even worse.

I didn't think Mum's silence would last long. 'It was a one night stand,' she said feebly.

Janet looked at me but I just shrugged. There was really nothing more I could say.

Sorry, Zygote, I thought to myself. *Hello and goodbye*.

But in spite of all that, Janet sent us home without signing any forms or making any appointments or doing that dreaded internal examination Mum warned me she might do.

'There's time,' she told us when she'd worked out the

date of my last period and how many weeks pregnant I probably was. I'd also had to produce a specimen of urine for a third test *and* given blood for a routine HIV scan. Mum was horrified at that. The thought I might have got Aids as well as pregnant almost gave her a cardiac arrest.

'How much time?' I asked, getting in before Mum could open her mouth.

'Up to twelve weeks,' Janet told me. 'So there's time to give it a bit more thought. Panic decisions are not the best ones. Talk about it, think about it. I'll make you an appointment with a c—'

'Clinic?' Mum said. 'I thought she could go to the NHS hospital.'

'No, not a clinic,' Janet said patiently. 'I was going to say I'd make her an appointment with a counsellor if she'd like to talk to someone about it.'

'Right,' said Mum on my behalf.

'Is that all right, Cass?' Janet ignored Mum and gazed at me through her tinted windows.

I shrugged again. 'I suppose so,' I mumbled. I seemed to be retreating inside myself . . . becoming like Alice when she found that '*drink me*' bottle and shrunk to almost nothing.

I was too miserable to say any more. I'd wanted it to be all over in this one visit. Arrangements made, forms filled in, surgical instruments ready . . . the dirty deed done. All over, put behind me, start again. I'd wanted Janet to write out a prescription for a magic potion that would simply make it disappear. But a counsellor? That was really the last thing I wanted. What was the point? Nothing would make any difference. This was between me and the zygote. Not Mum, not Dad, not anyone else in the world.

As far as I was concerned the worst thing that could ever happen had happened and I might as well be dead.

So we drove back home. Mum at the wheel. Tight-lipped, pale, silent. Me slumped in the front seat staring at the grey world flashing past.

'Drop me off at the park,' I said when we'd gone past Tesco's and Texas and all the superstores south of town. 'I want to be by myself.'

Mum looked at me, then quickly back at the road as a rager honked his horn at us for going too slow. 'You won't do anything silly?'

'Don't be daft,' I said even though suicide *had* vaguely flitted through my imagination in the dark days when I was the only one who knew what was happening to me. Now, though, it was the zygote's termination we were contemplating—not mine. 'I just want to think, that's all,' I told her miserably.

She pulled up by the park gates. When I looked at her she was pale and drawn, dark shadows under her eyes. I noticed for the first time that she had grey hairs amongst the black ones. Had I put them there? Was it because of me she was going grey at thirty-six? I felt sorry for her and guilty that I was causing all the hassle. In fact I felt worse than I had ever done, or expected to feel for the rest of my life.

'I'm sorry, Mum,' I said.

She had tears in her eyes. 'These things happen.' She sighed. A huge deep sigh as if she had inhaled all the troubles of the world. 'If only you'd told me earlier.'

'How could I have told you?' I said. I couldn't look at her so I fiddled with the zip on my jacket. 'You'd have gone—'

'Mad?' she said. 'Probably. But it would have been better than this.'

She was right. Anything would have been better than this.

'Now,' Mum went on. 'I just want it over and done with for all our sakes. Before it becomes more than just a bunch of cells . . . '

'A zygote,' I said.

'A what?' She gazed at me.

'A zygote . . . that's what it's called.'

'Oh,' she said. 'Well, whatever it's called we must tell

Janet we haven't changed our minds quickly before it becomes a—' She stopped abruptly and when I looked at her I could see her eyes were filled with moisture.

'Don't you fancy being a gran?' I said lightly.

I don't know what made me say it. For some horrible reason I wanted to hurt her. Hurt everyone I came into contact with. My pain and sorrow were reflected in her eyes. Her knuckles were white against the steering wheel. 'Cass,' she said. 'I'm just beginning to do all the things I've wanted to do for years. It would be different if you'd been in a steady relationship . . . if we'd known the father. But you weren't and we don't and there's no way you could manage a baby on your own. It would be me who had to look after it while you finish your education and I want more out of life now.'

'Yes,' I said feebly, looking down at my knees.

'Every child should be loved and wanted,' she said. 'Like you were.'

'Yes,' I said just as feebly. I didn't know who she was trying to convince—me or her.

'I've spent sixteen years looking after you and Dad and the house,' she rattled on. 'Now I want to do things for myself.'

'For yourself?' I said.

The years she had spent devoting herself to the family suddenly loomed up in front of me. How selfish we were, taking it for granted she'd always be there for us.

'Yes,' she said, still gripping the wheel. 'Me. In years to come, when you get married, it'll be different. I'll be ready then.'

'Married!' I screwed up my nose. 'You've got to be joking.'

She was still gazing at me. 'Yes, Cass. Married. Some people do still do it, you know.'

'I'm sorry,' I said again. I seemed to be saying it a lot lately.

Sorry I was stupid.

Sorry I'm causing so much grief.

26

Sorry I'm pregnant.

Sorry, Mum.

Sorry, Dad.

Sorry, zygote.

Tears blurred my selfishness as I fumbled for the door handle and flung myself from the car.

I sat down on one of the park benches. It was still damp with morning dew but I didn't really care. The sun had come out, suddenly appearing from the edge of a dark cloud and shedding an arc of brightness across the grass. A squirrel ran down from an oak tree and sat a metre away from me, an acorn held in its little paws. He seemed to be looking around for a place to hide it. I guessed that with the start of the chill autumn days he'd decided to start his store of winter food. I held my breath, feeling glad he wasn't scared to sit so close to me. That he'd chosen me to not be afraid of. Then suddenly he scampered away sending up little fountains of fallen leaves as he ran. I sighed as the strange, magic spell he had cast round me was shattered.

Then I saw why he'd scarpered. Coming along the path and heading straight for me was animal James Derwent. I swore under my breath. A fat pig from school was the last person in the world I wanted to see.

Worse still, he'd spotted me and was jogging up the bank towards me.

'Wotcha, Cass.'

I looked up, screwing my eyes up against the sun. I hated James Derwent. He's about a ton overweight and hardly ever without some junk food or other stuffed in his mouth. Him and his mates cause havoc wherever they go. Which is mostly to the Head's office to be threatened with suspension.

I knew James lived on the estate behind the sports centre and has got about a million brothers and sisters who all live like pigs too. I'd ridden past his house on my bike once. Tatty front door, a couple of half dismembered rusting cars in the front garden, graffiti on the wall. *Mo woz here. You'll never walk alone. Manchester United.* A swastika. He'd got black, greasy hair and never wore anything but a tracksuit. I don't know why, because I'd never seen him playing any sports or doing anything in the school gym. I think he and his mates saw themselves as fashion icons instead of what they *really* were.

Prats.

Surprisingly though, James looked as if he'd been running. *Really* running, not just scarpering from some act of vandalism he'd just done. His tatty trainers were muddy and he'd got splashes all the way up the back of his tracksuit bottoms. He was sweating too . . . and he stank like the boys' changing room.

'Get lost,' I said which was about all I'd ever said to him in my life even though I'd known him since primary school.

But he ignored what I'd said and sat down beside me, still sweating and panting as though he'd run a marathon. I could feel the heat coming off him like a radiator.

'I'm getting in training,' he said.

'What for?' I answered. 'The circus?' I hated him being there. Hating his intrusion into my misery. In fact I hated everyone and everything. Especially myself.

'Very funny.' He wiped his sleeve across his sweaty forehead. 'I'm doing a sponsored run,' he explained even though I hadn't asked him to and didn't want to know anyway. I wasn't remotely interested in anything he'd got to say.

'Big deal.' I got up. 'Bye, James, don't overdo it, you might get a cardiac arrest.' *With a bit of luck*, I added to myself as I walked away.

He got up and followed me, scuffing through the leaves and sending up little eruptions of them with his clumsy great feet.

28

'What you doing here all by yourself?'

'Nothing.' I walked faster hoping he'd scarper.

'Weird thing to do,' he said, jogging along beside me. 'Sitting on a park bench doing nothing.' He was just too gross to appreciate that sometimes people needed time and space to think.

I looked at him. At his dark eyes and floppy hair. 'What's it to you?'

He shrugged. 'Nothing. You just looked peed off that's all.'

'Just get lost, James,' I said, hating him more than ever.

So he did.

I watched him jog away, down the slope, past the pond and on to the path that went round the edge of the park. He almost slammed into a woman pushing a pram coming the other way. I saw him trip and hop and fling some abuse at her then disappear behind the pavilion.

I watched her trundle the buggy towards the pond. She looked quite old to have a young kid. Then I realized she was probably its grandmother. I thought about my own gran who died last year. She'd been a great traveller. Going off on trips all over the place. Australia. India . . . the Far East, America. She'd even trekked up the Himalayas with a group of guys years younger than herself.

'You're mad,' Dad said to her every time she made new plans even though I knew secretly he was proud of her. My dad was too conventional, that was the trouble. Too ordinary. *His* dad had been the same, Gran told me. In Dad's eyes, grans should wear cardigans and brown tights and babysit when you needed them. But she had always shaken her head when he went on at her.

'I want to live before I die,' she told him.

Suddenly, thinking of her, the world blurred and I began to cry again. I couldn't help it. Salt burning my skin. What would she think of me now? A dead loss, I reckoned. I really miss her. Her traveller's tales, her

photos of great and wonderful places. I wanted to do all
that stuff too. I didn't want to wait sixty years like she'd
had to. I wanted to do them as soon as I could.

'Don't be in too much of a hurry,' she'd said when I
told her how I felt. 'The world won't go away and it
looks better through the eyes of experience.'

I didn't even wipe the tears away. Right then, the
world looked terrible through *my* eyes of experience.

A group of men with children came through the gate.
They headed for the pond. They had toy sailing boats
under their arms and were chattering and laughing
excitedly. I wanted to join in, to be a kid again. I hated
my body being old enough to have another one growing
inside it. I'd wanted so much to be grown up. Now all I
wanted was to be young again.

Then I spotted animal James coming my way again.
He'd jogged the whole perimeter of the park and was
back, heading towards me like a herd of elephants.

I simply couldn't stand it if he saw me crying.

So I ran.

4

'You been crying?' James asked when he caught me up.
I should have known I couldn't hide it.

I sniffed and rubbed my nose with my sleeve and lied.
'No, 'course not, don't be stupid.'

He was looking at me, right in the eye as if he could
see into my head. 'Perhaps you've got an allergy,' he
said. 'My kid brother's allergic to everything.'

'It's you I'm allergic to,' I told him. 'So for God's
sake get lost.'

But he still jogged along beside me all the way to the
park gates. I decided he was deaf . . . or really thick . . .
or both.

I sighed. 'For God's sake, James, why don't you just
bog off?' I was being even more horrible than even *I*
thought I could be.

He held up his hands. 'OK, OK, sorry I spoke.'

Then I felt guilty again. James might be a yob but for
once in his life he was trying to be friendly. It wasn't his
fault I was feeling like a funeral.

I sighed. 'Look, James, I'm sorry. I'm just in a bad
mood, that's all.'

He shrugged and raised his eyebrows but didn't say
anything.

'What are you in training for anyway?' I asked in a
fairly civilized voice to try to make up for my
beastliness.

By now we'd gone through the park gates and were
waiting to cross the road. It was Saturday and cars were
streaming out of the supermarket and on to the ring-road.

'I'm doing a sponsored run,' he said. 'One of my sisters is trying to raise money to send this kid in our road to America for a brain operation.'

'Blimey,' I said. 'It's not like you. Doing good deeds.'

He looked hurt and almost human for a minute. Maybe he only turned into an animal when he was at school.

He shrugged. 'It gets me out of the house.'

I had a sudden vision of what it must be like living in one of those squalid places with all those kids. I wasn't even sure how many there were. I only knew that two others besides James were at our school.

'That's good, is it?' I asked as the man went green and we crossed over.

'What? Getting out of the house. You kidding?' he said. 'It's a zoo.'

We were walking past the video shop and the mini-market. Inside, people were queuing up to get their lottery tickets. Everyone wanted today to be the day that changed their lives. Me included.

'Don't you get on with your mum and dad?' I asked.

He shrugged. 'My mum's all right but my old man's a pig.' He didn't say any more. He just snorted air through his nostrils that said more than any words.

'Oh?' was all I could think of to say.

James chewed on his lip as he glanced at his watch. 'I'd better go. Mum's got to go to work.'

'So?' I said stupidly.

'So the little ones will be on their own,' he said.

'Oh,' I said feebly. Somehow I'd never seen him in the role of babysitter. I'd never really seen him as anything except a pain in the neck. 'Isn't your dad there?'

He shook his head. 'He goes down the pub,' he said.

'Oh,' I said again.

'See ya,' James said.

'Not if I see you first,' I said, meaning it as a joke even though it didn't really come out like that.

He dived across the road, hardly looking where he was going. A bus screeched to a halt, missing him by a few centimetres. The driver shouted something from the window. James stuck his fingers up, dived down the alley between the Body Shop and W. H. Smith and disappeared.

I stood there watching the space where he'd been. Then the shoppers folded in and even that disappeared. I turned away and headed for home. I really had got too many problems of my own to worry about someone like James Derwent.

At home I decided to phone Mel. She sounded really pleased to hear me. I told her about our visit to the doc's.

'Surely she doesn't think you'd *want* to keep it,' she said in a stunned, horror-movie voice.

'She's mad if she does,' I said. 'But I suppose she just thought I should take a bit longer to think about it.'

Mel snorted. 'What? Like about five seconds.'

I chuckled even though it wasn't funny. In fact I didn't think I'd ever find anything funny again.

'When are you going back?' Mel asked.

'Next week,' I told her. 'Thursday. I can't wait.' It sounded such a long way away . . . a lifetime of misery squashed into a few days.

'Then what?' Mel was asking.

'I don't know.'

'Didn't you ask?'

'No. There didn't seem to be much point.'

'Oh?' I could tell Mel was surprised. If it had been her she'd have wanted to know everything there and then, down to the very last sordid detail. 'Well,' she went on. 'She'll tell you when you go I guess.'

'Yes,' I said lamely.

'Aren't you scared?'

''Course I am,' I told her. 'I'm petrified.'

That was the first time I'd admitted that. Even to myself. What did they do to you when you got an abortion? Did they cut your stomach open and take the zygote out? I wished I'd asked the first time so at least I'd know what to expect when the day of execution came.

'If it was me,' Mel was rattling on as if she was telepathic and knew what I was thinking, 'I'd go back on my own. I couldn't stand my mum interfering.'

'Yes,' I said thoughtfully. 'In fact, I think I might just do that.'

On Monday, school was an absolute nightmare. I couldn't concentrate on anything. Between lessons I phoned the surgery to make an earlier appointment. Tomorrow, they said. Morning surgery. 10 o'clock. I began counting the minutes.

At break, Mel pulled my sleeve. 'I've found out,' she said, dragging me towards the girls' loos. James Derwent and his mates were stampeding down the corridor like a charge of rhinos towards us. He was with them but lagging behind for a change. I took a deep breath. If he said anything about me being in the park I'd kill him.

But all he said in passing was, 'You OK?'

'Yes, thanks,' I lied.

At the door he turned and gave me a vampire stare before one of the others shoved him through and slammed it behind them.

Luckily there was no one else in the cloakroom. Mel pulled a booklet from her bag. 'Termination—methods and recovery,' it said on the front.

'Where did you get that?' I eyed it curiously.

'It was in Sharon's file,' Mel told me. Sharon, her sister, was training to be a nurse. 'I suddenly had this brainwave that there might be something in there because she told me she's doing gynaecology.'

I took it from her and thumbed through the pages.

It was all there. Methods, after effects, facts and figures. We pored over it in silence.

'Looks simple to me,' Mel said when we'd scanned the details. 'Nothing to worry about.'

I swallowed. 'Yeah,' I said. 'Simple when it's someone else.'

Mel put her arm round me and rested her temple against mine. 'Sorry, Cass, I'm just trying to cheer you up. It's not that unusual, you know.' She pointed. 'Look at these statistics.'

I scanned the page. 'Over one hundred and eighty-one thousand abortions were performed in the United Kingdom last year.' *One hundred and eighty-one thousand!* I couldn't get my head around a figure like that.

Mel could. Mel never had any trouble getting her head round anything. I got the feeling that if it was her in the same boat she'd just go off cheerfully to the hospital thinking of it as a mere hiccup in her life's master plan.

'There you are, you see,' she said. 'It's no big deal.'

I stared at her. She didn't understand at all. She thought it was simply an operation. Like having your tooth out or your tonsils, or cutting your toenails. She had no idea what it felt like to have another person growing inside you. How it made you feel horrible and stupid and ill. But then, how could she? How could anyone know until it happened to them.

Suddenly I didn't want to talk about it any more.

I got up. 'Thanks for finding out,' I said. 'I've got to go now.'

I grabbed my bag and left her staring at me as if I'd dematerialized into absolutely nothing at all.

'Now, you are completely sure, aren't you?' Doctor Janet said when I went to the surgery the following morning. To my absolute horror I burst into tears when she asked me that. I'd thought my ocean of weeping had dried up.

To make things worse, I'd had to spend ages in the waiting room. I'd told my tutor I'd be late getting to school. I'd said my mum had got flu and I'd got to get some shopping. I felt awful. I'd never lied about anything like that before. I felt awful too about not telling Mum I was going to the doc, but it was just something I had to do by myself. There was no way I could have her there answering the doc's questions for me as if I was still her little girl.

The waiting room had been chock-a-block with patients. Worse still, James Derwent's mum was sitting there with a black eye. I knew it was her because I remembered seeing her once at junior school when she came to watch a school play. James had been playing Humpty Dumpty, surprise, surprise. Even though she'd got her face stuffed in a *Chat* magazine I saw the bruise around her eye when she glanced up as I came in. I wondered how she got it. Bumped into a door? Fallen over? I remembered James's angry face when he mentioned his dad and got a horrible feeling inside me.

She had a grubby baby in a grubby buggy. It kept sneezing and snot ran down into its mouth. She kept tutting and leaning forward to wipe it with an already soggy tissue. The other kid played with a toy train on the floor. He kept bashing into an old man's leg but she didn't tell him off. I got the feeling he wouldn't have taken any notice of her if she had.

The first thing Janet asked me when my name had been called was if I'd thought any more about Mum's/my decision.

'You're absolutely sure?' she said when I told her.

I gazed at her. 'Positive,' I said.

'You've discussed it with your parents again?'

'No,' I admitted. 'But there's no need. You heard what Mum said.'

She sighed. 'I want *you* to say it, Cass.'

'OK, then,' I sniffed. 'I've said it. Anyway, lots of women have it done, don't they?'

She stared at me. 'Yes, of course they do, Cass. Some for different reasons from you, though.'

I hadn't thought about that before. I'd been so busy thinking about myself I'd never given a thought to people who got abortions for other reasons. If the baby was ill or not formed properly. I realized how awful it must be to have to decide such a terrible thing.

I hung my head. 'Yes,' I mumbled. 'I suppose so.'

She leaned forward. 'Had you thought about having the baby adopted, Cass?'

I closed my eyes. I wished she wouldn't say the word 'baby'. It wasn't a baby, it was a zygote. Surely she knew that?

I gulped. 'Adopted?'

'Yes, there are thousands and thousands—'

I shook my head. 'No!'

Not for one minute had I thought about adoption. But now I did, I knew I could never do it. The thought of going through all that then giving up the— I knew I simply couldn't.

'No,' I repeated. 'No way . . .'

She sighed again. 'OK, Cass.' She took a form from the drawer. 'I'll make you an appointment at the hospital.'

'Right,' I croaked. 'What will they say to me there?'

'You'll see a counsellor first.' She frowned as she filled in the form. Then she tapped something on her computer keyboard and pressed enter.

I gazed at the screen in horror.

'Will it be on my records?' I said in a kind of strangled voice. I didn't think I could bear it if doctors for ever more knew how stupid I'd been and what I'd done.

'Not if you don't want it to,' she said.

'No,' I answered. 'I don't . . . definitely.'

She made another note on the screen.

'What will the counsellor say?' I wanted to know, still hating the idea of talking about it. Especially to a stranger.

'She'll tell you about the abortion . . . methods . . . what they'll do. She'll answer any questions you might have and discuss what you'll do afterwards.'

'Afterwards?' I frowned.

'Yes,' she said. 'You'll need a while to get over things.'

I shook my head. 'No, I won't,' I told her. 'I'll just carry on like it never happened.'

She gave me a funny look but didn't say any more.

I didn't tell her I already knew from Sharon's book about what they did to you at the hospital. I knew there were several methods but vacuum aspiration was the one they'd most likely use. That was where they give you a general anaesthetic and put in a tube and suck the zygote out. I felt sick at the thought. Being pregnant made you sick. Getting an abortion made you sick too. I couldn't wait for it to be all over.

'Can't they just do it there and then and get it over with?' I said.

She shook her head. 'Everyone has counselling and we have to have the agreement of another doctor.'

'Why's that?' My heart lurched and I felt sicker than ever. What other doctor? Supposing she or he wouldn't agree? Then what would happen?

'It's the law,' she said. 'Two doctors have to give their consent.' She leaned forward. 'We have to certify that continuing with the pregnancy will be bad for your physical and mental health. Don't worry, it won't be a problem.'

'Good,' I said, thinking of the one hundred and eighty-one thousand whose physical and mental health had been threatened.

'They won't try to make me change my mind?' I asked.

She shook her head. 'No, of course not. They won't try to make you do anything. The final decision is up to you.'

I was grateful for that. The first time anyone had treated me like a real person since the nightmare started.

She leaned further forward. 'But if you do, Cass, don't be afraid to tell them.'

'Don't worry . . . ' I got up and picked up my school bag. 'I won't.'

'And when it's all over,' she added as I hovered on the threshold, anxious to be gone, 'come to me for some contraceptive advice or go to the family planning clinic, OK?'

'OK,' I choked. She had got to be joking. I was never going to have sex with anyone ever again.

I lurched out into the grey day. It was raining, fine misty droplets quivered from every bare branch. The sort of day when you know that summer has gone for ever.

The pavement was soggy with leaves. The sky looked leaden and as heavy as my heart. I didn't think I could face going to school so I turned and headed for town. Hopefully Mrs Brown would think I'd got flu too.

McDonald's was almost empty. An old tramp sat in one corner studying the Ronald McDonald placemat as if it was *War and Peace*. A man in a business suit sat by children's corner with a Big Mac and what looked like a vanilla milk shake. He had a laptop computer and was busily keying in notes in between bites of his burger bun. I saw him drop a bit on the keyboard and try to fish it out from between the T and the Y with the end of his plastic stirrer.

I got a regular Coke and sat down, huddled in the corner where I hoped I would be so small that no one would be able to see me. Grey people went past the window, grey umbrellas up, grey shopping bags clutched in damp hands. In fact the whole outside world was grey. I wondered about all those people. Some, like me, seemed to be carrying the world on their shoulders. Others walked briskly, in a hurry or just full of the energy of living. I wondered what their lives were like . . . did they have to make decisions like mine? Did they carry on with their existence as if the end of the world wasn't about to happen?

I heard a clatter and a toddler yelling something and to my horror Mrs Derwent came through the door with her two kids and her black eye. I couldn't believe it. That family was haunting my wildest nightmares.

She sat the elder of the children down in the red and blue play-train in kiddies' corner, threatened it with death, stuck the buggy against the table next to mine and went to order something at the counter. Coming back, she noticed me sitting there.

She shoved an ice cream at the child on the train and came to sit beside me.

'You're at Jamie's school, aren't you?' she said. She peeled the lid off her polystyrene cup and emptied two packets of sugar into her tea. She stirred it absent-mindedly.

Jamie? Somehow I couldn't think of James Derwent as ever being called *Jamie*.

'Yes.' I swallowed. Why, today of all days, did I have to meet her?

'You were in the doctor's.'

When I looked at her I saw she had other bruises. One behind her ear, the other on her arm, four marks like fingers dug in deep. I suddenly went cold. As if someone had sliced a bit off my head with an ice scalpel. Someone had bashed her and it didn't take much brain to guess it had probably been James's dad. I felt a sudden, hopeless, rush of pity.

I swallowed. 'Yes,' I said again like a robot programmed to say only one word.

'You sick, then?' She took a sip of her tea then swore because it was so hot.

I shrugged. 'Not really,' I fibbed.

'Bunking off school, then?' she asked.

I shrugged again. 'Kind of.'

'I threatened James,' she said. 'If he bunks off I'll murder him. The only hope he's got is getting good exam results.'

In your dreams, I said to myself. Surely she must know how her darling son behaved at school.

'That's what my mum says,' I heard someone saying prissily then realized it was me. 'About me, I mean,' I added hastily in case she thought I was talking about James.

She gazed at me. 'Shouldn't think you have any trouble,' she said. 'You look brainy.'

I heard a loud laugh and realized *that* was coming from me as well. I felt suddenly as if someone else had invaded my head. Talking, making gestures that somehow had nothing to do with me at all. It must have been the old Cass, the one who hadn't been stupid enough to get pregnant. 'How can anyone look brainy?'

She smiled too and I suddenly saw where James got his dark blue eyes from.

'Oh,' she said, 'you can just tell.'

If she knew what I knew then she wouldn't think I was brainy at all—brain*less* more like.

She sat silently stirring her tea.

'Do you know my Jamie?' she asked suddenly.

'Er . . . yeah,' I said. 'Everyone knows James.'

She sighed. 'Yes, I bet.' Suddenly, her eyes were bright with tears. 'I do my best, you know . . . it's not easy.'

The other me felt another sudden, violent surge of compassion. That vision of her grotty house and all those kids rose up in front of me like some ghastly horror movie. It was on the tip of my tongue to ask her where she got her black eye, even though I'd got that horrible feeling I already knew.

The baby in the pushchair suddenly woke up and began to cry. Mrs D. leaned forward, undid the waterproof apron and dragged the baby out. She wiped its face with a McDonald's paper napkin. Now it was out of the pram I could see it was a girl. She had a sweet face and dark curls. She suddenly stopped crying and stared solemnly at me with big blue eyes.

'There, that's better, Alice,' Mrs D. cooed.

'How old is she?' I asked before I could stop myself.

'Nine months,' Mrs D. said. Then she smiled. 'She's my granddaughter . . . my eldest, Lizzie, she's hers.'

'Oh,' I said.

'There's only two years between her and Shaun,' she said indicating the sticky toddler. He had got out of the train and was kicking hell out of the wheels. Mrs D. just let him get on with it. 'Funny having a son and a granddaughter practically the same age.'

'Yes,' I said again, thinking she was right. It was really weird.

The baby was still staring at me then suddenly she held out her arms towards me. I sat back in horror. Surely she didn't want me to pick her up?

'Go on,' Mrs Derwent said. 'She won't bite.'

So although I didn't know why, I took Alice on to my lap.

She smiled up at me and tried to fiddle with the zip on my coat. She smelt a bit. Of cornflakes and cheese and onion crisps and some other nameless thing. *And* she still had a runny nose. But strangely I didn't mind a bit. Then she pulled at one of my ear-rings.

I prised her gently away. Her hand lay in mine, perfect grubby finger nails, little creases, her little finger like a tiny pink worm. She snuggled up against me, warm and cuddly, put her thumb into her mouth and closed her eyes.

Mrs Derwent laughed. 'You've got a magic touch.'

Suddenly I couldn't bear it. I handed her back to her gran. I'd never held such a young kid before and it gave me a really weird feeling. As if she knew, and I knew, she was safe in my arms. I must seem big to her. A giant. All grown-ups must seem like giants. Maybe that's why kids like stories about giants . . . everyone's one to them.

I swallowed. 'I've got to go,' I mumbled. I was

suddenly me again. That other strange person who had taken over my head had fled away.

I grabbed my bag and ran.

I almost tripped as I hurtled away from them. The old tramp looked up from his blockbuster placemat in surprise. He frowned as I ran towards the door. Mrs Derwent was probably startled too but I didn't look round to find out. And even if I had, my eyes would have been too blurred to see.

5

The appointment with the hospital came through a day or so after I went to the doctor's on my own. Friday, 29th, someone had written on a dotted line in the middle of a printed letter.

Friday, 29th. It was branded on my brain.

Mum was getting breakfast when the post came.

I wanted to hide away the letter, not let anyone know, but I knew I couldn't do that so I showed it to Mum.

'Have you been back to the doctor already, then?' She stared at me in surprise.

Dad was there. He was catching a later train that day. He looked up from the paper.

'Yes.' I sat down and leaned my elbows on the table.

'You could have told me,' Mum said, hurt.

I shrugged. 'There wasn't any point. I just wanted to tell Janet I hadn't changed my mind and to get me an appointment at the hospital as soon as she could. So that's what she's done.'

Mum and Dad exchanged glances.

'What did she say to you?' Mum asked.

I shrugged again. 'Nothing much . . . she . . . '

'What?' Mum asked.

'She said, had I thought about adoption.'

'Adoption?' Mum frowned. 'Oh, Cass. It would be terrible to have a . . . a baby then give it up. You can't imagine how you would feel.'

Dad was shaking his head. 'Terrible,' he murmured. 'Terrible, you've no idea, Cass.'

I stared at them. 'Of course I know how it would

feel,' I said, trying not to shout. 'I'm not stupid . . . I do have feelings, you know.'

Mum patted my hand. 'Yes, of course, we know you do. But you're only sixteen—' she broke off, knowing she had said that once too often.

'I *know* I'm only sixteen,' I shouted. 'You remind me every day.'

'Cass, don't talk to your mother like that.' Dad came down on me like a ton of bricks.

But Mum waved her hand. 'I'm sorry, Cass,' she said.

'No you're not,' I was really yelling now. 'You think I'm still a baby. You think I don't have feelings like any other woman.'

Mum was looking upset and shaking her head. 'That's not true, Cass.'

I got up. I wanted to run. Run and run. Out of the house, out of the world.

'It doesn't make any difference *how* old I am,' I hissed. 'I've got the same feelings as anyone else.'

Dad flung out his hand and pulled me back down. 'We know you have, Cass. Please . . . try to calm down.'

I plonked myself in the chair. 'How can I calm down when you go on treating me like a child.'

'We're sorry, aren't we, Mum?' Dad looked at her, frowning.

'Yes,' she said. 'Honestly, Cass.'

Dad leaned towards me. 'Do you want Mum to go with you to the hospital?' He sighed as relative normality was restored.

Nothing was further from my mind. 'No.'

Mum. 'Cass, you can't go by yourself. What will people think?'

'I don't care what they think!' I was shouting again. 'I'm going by myself and that's that. I don't *need* anyone there. I'll be OK.'

I didn't know why I was telling so many fibs. It was as if it had got to be a habit.

'Cass, you're shutting us out,' Mum said with one of her famous, well practised sighs of resignation.

Hair shrouded my face. 'I know, I can't help it. I'm sorry.'

It was true. I seemed to have sunk right down into a black pit and couldn't get out. If I couldn't shrivel up and disappear I might as well drown.

'You'll feel better when it's over,' Dad leaned across to pat my hand. 'You're bound to feel depressed.'

'Yes,' I mumbled. 'If you say so, Dad.'

'Will that be it then?' he asked, talking to me but looking at Mum. 'Will she have the . . . operation there and then?'

'No,' I said.

He looked confused. 'What do you mean, no?'

'What I say,' I told him. 'You have to talk to someone, then make another appointment.'

'God,' Mum said. 'How many more?' The toast popped out with a clang. She got up to fetch it, slamming it on to a plate and crashing it down on the table.

I got up. I couldn't stand any more of their stupid questions. It really was time to run.

'I don't *know*,' I yelled. 'I don't know, I don't know. For God's sake leave me alone!'

I flung out of the room, grabbed my coat and bag and slammed the front door behind me. I could imagine them looking at each other and sighing hopelessly. Where had they gone wrong? they'd be wondering. Where on earth had they gone wrong? Except it wasn't them who had gone wrong at all.

It was me.

I seemed to be going round in a trance after that. One word kept pounding through my brain like the last bit of music you hear before you go to bed. It keeps spinning round and round in your head like a never-ending CD.

Friday . . . Friday . . . Friday.

It couldn't come round soon enough for me.

46

'Have you told anyone?' Mum asked when I got home from school that evening. She seemed to have forgotten the row we'd had at breakfast.

'Don't be daft,' I said. 'It's not exactly something you go around bragging about.' I couldn't help fibbing. They would hate it if they knew I'd even told Mel.

Tight lipped, she commented, 'No, I suppose not,' in a kind of strangled voice. Then she said, 'I'm going to write Mrs Brown a note, tell her you need Friday off.'

I need the rest of my life off, I thought but didn't say it.

'Thanks,' I mumbled grudgingly.

That night I had a strange dream. I hadn't even thought I would sleep but I must have dozed off eventually.

I was swimming through thick, oily water. My arms and legs were so heavy I could hardly move them. I was getting nowhere. On either side were steep banks. One side had blue sky, green fields, flowers, people having a great time. The other side was grey and dismal. People walked with their heads down, tired, depressed, shoulders hunched against the drizzle. They were all women, scarved and dowdy, weighed down with the hopelessness of unfulfilled promises. I kept trying to steer myself towards the green fields but felt myself being drawn towards the opposite side. It was strange but all the time it was happening I knew it was only a dream.

I suddenly woke with a jump. I opened my eyes wide against the darkness. The clock said gone midnight. Through a gap in the curtains I could see the moon, white and clear. In the distance a dog barked. I got up to go to the loo. In the bathroom I caught sight of myself in the mirror. Bleary eyed, pale . . . thin, hair like rats' tails. If I didn't pull myself together soon I'd end up looking like a sixteen-year-old hag.

I stared at my reflection then lifted up the old T-shirt

47

I wore as a nightie and stared some more. I put my hand on my stomach. It was still flat as a pancake, hipbones sticking out. It seemed impossible another human being was growing inside there . . . I was still thinking I might wake from some terrible nightmare. Yet three tests couldn't be wrong. Morning sickness couldn't be wrong. My reflection fogged as if I was about to be turned into something else. I wiped away the tear that bubbled from my eye and crawled back to bed.

Mum and Dad were still up. I could hear them arguing in the front room.

I stopped to listen. I used to do that when I was small. I remember crouching there, listening to their rows, heart beating in terror. There's nothing worse in the world than hearing your parents fight.

'You left it up to me,' Mum was saying. 'Now you're saying you're not sure it's the right decision. That's typical of you.'

There was silence for a second or two. Then Dad said, 'I'm just saying she hasn't really had time to think about it, that's all. We haven't even told her that if she decides to keep it we'll give her our support. I mean . . . poor kid.'

'You mean *I'll* give my support,' Mum said angrily.

'Both of us,' Dad answered.

'So you'll change nappies and wake up in the night to feed it, will you?' Mum shouted. 'You'll take it to the shops, the park . . . nursery . . . ? You'll devote your life to it?'

'Oh, please, Karen,' Dad sighed. 'Cass will still be its mother.'

Its mother, its mother . . . me a mother. I couldn't get my head round that. I really didn't want to hear any more but something kept me glued there.

'You can't be a proper mother when you're at school all day,' Mum was saying. 'And she can't give up her education, it will break all our hearts.'

'No one's suggesting she should,' Dad said. I could tell by his voice he knew he was losing.

'No, and that means I'd be the one to look after it.' I could imagine Mum leaning towards him tapping her chest. 'And I want a life of my own now, Brian. Is that too much to ask?'

'I just hoped we'd have grandchildren one day, that was all,' my dad said lamely.

A knife twisted in my heart as Mum burst into tears. 'One day, of course,' she sobbed. 'But not now, Brian, it's too soon. Cass isn't ready and neither am I. For goodness' sake, she's hardly more than a baby herself.'

'But she isn't a baby any more, Karen,' I heard my dad say. 'And we've got to realize it whether we like it or not.'

My mum didn't answer and all I could hear was the sound of her weeping.

I heard my dad say something softly then there was silence.

I crept back to my room. Curled up under the duvet, small like the kernel of a nut, and cried myself back to sleep.

In the morning they were both in a foul mood. So was I. Breakfast was like one of those mime shows. Dad waved his hand for the toast. I waved mine for the marmalade. It was the first time since I'd got pregnant that I'd felt remotely like breakfast. That scared me. I mean *really* scared me. It meant my pregnancy was entering another stage. That my body was getting used to the alien creature growing inside it.

That day I'd got no intention of going to school although I didn't let on. There was no way I could face it. I couldn't concentrate anyway. Maths added up to nothing, English was all double Dutch. Science was a mystery and Art just a jumble of colours and shapes that didn't mean a thing. I'd soon get back into the swing of things, I tried to convince myself. When it was all over.

I left at the usual time, headed towards the bus stop in case Mum was looking out of the window then turned towards town. I didn't know what I was going to do with myself until four o'clock.

The hours stretched endlessly ahead. I could go to McDonald's, the library, the sports centre. I could jump in the canal, dive from the multi-storey, stand in the fast lane of the motorway. I was just wandering aimlessly along the pavement when footsteps pounded behind me and Dracula turned up. If I hadn't known better I'd have said he'd been hanging about waiting for me.

'Get lost, James,' I said as usual.

He was panting and had obviously been training for his sponsored run. Without answering he dragged a grimy form from his pocket.

'Will you sponsor me, Cass?'

I sighed. 'Do I have to?'

'It could save a kid's life.'

I stared at him. This really was a new James Derwent. Was it my imagination or had he washed his hair? And he was losing weight. If he didn't watch out he might even get to be remotely attractive.

I sighed again. 'OK, how much?'

He shrugged. 'Whatever you like.'

I got a pen from my bag and scribbled down two quid under a dozen or so names and a variety of sums from ten pence to three quid on the list.

'Aren't your mates sponsoring you?' I asked as I handed him back his pen and the form. I'd noticed none of their names were on there.

He shrugged again. 'They think I'm stupid. Anyway, they're not my mates any more.'

'Oh?' I spluttered, not believing him. 'Since when?'

'I just got peed off with them, that's all.' He stuffed the form back into his pocket.

'You sure it's not the other way round?' I said.

He grinned. 'Half and half,' he said. 'Trouble is, it's not easy to get yourself out of a situation once you're in it.'

This seemed a strangely profound statement coming from someone like him.

'You're not kidding,' I said.

'Anyway,' he went on and his face took on that hard look I'd seen before, 'my old man had to go up the school again. He hates going up there. He hated his own school and now he hates mine. Hates the teachers too. He hates everything really—me especially.'

'I'm sure that's not true,' I said stupidly.

He looked at me. 'He said he'd kill me if I got into any more trouble.'

'Yeah?' I stared back at him. Something like fear was in his eyes. I'd never seen that before. In my book James Derwent wasn't scared of anything or anybody

'Yeah . . . and he means it,' James said.

By now, we were in the High Street.

'You bunking off again?' he asked me.

I nodded.

'Getting to be a habit, isn't it?' he said.

I just shrugged.

'Fancy a Coke?'

I hesitated. Then I nodded. After all, what else was there to do?

We sat in silence. The café was empty except for us.

'What did you mean when you said about not being able to get yourself out of a situation?' I asked him halfway through my drink. I'd been turning his words over in my mind.

'What I say,' he answered.

'I mean, what situation?'

'Well, like, getting in with those guys, feeling you've got to do what they do so they'll like you. It's not easy to get friends when you're someone like me. You have to make out you're just like them even if you're not.'

'Does it really matter?' I asked. I felt puzzled. I didn't particularly care if people liked me or not.

'Yeah.' He looked at me. ''Course it does. It's all

right for you. You're good looking, you've got brains. *You* live in Kingsmere,' he added with a sneer.

Everyone who *didn't* live in Kingsmere thought it was posh. It was really just an ordinary estate full of ordinary people, even though it was a world away from where he lived.

But it was the other things he'd said that sounded really crazy.

I began to giggle. 'Good looking? Me? You need glasses, if you ask me.'

'No I don't,' he said.

I noticed he'd gone red so I said something else quickly. I wasn't sure why it had suddenly become important not to embarrass James Derwent.

'So go on,' I said. 'Tell me why it's so important to be one of the gang.'

'So you don't get bullied.' He looked down at the table.

'Bullied,' I chuckled. What on earth was he talking about. *He* was the one who was the bully. 'You?' I snorted.

'Yeah,' he answered, fiddling with one of the packets of sugar. 'Me.'

He told me then. How he'd been pushed around at junior school, how it had carried on at the high school. It had only been since he'd got in with his rough mates that he really felt safe . . . protected.

'They came from Brookworth,' he said meaning a tough junior school on the other side of the town, 'so they didn't know me before. Because I was big they thought I was tough.'

'And aren't you?' I stared at him, narrowing my eyes as if it would make me see better.

He dropped his gaze. 'Not really,' he said.

I suddenly realized that was what I thought too. What everyone thought. I suddenly felt horribly sorry for James Derwent, something I thought I'd never be.

Abruptly, he changed the subject.

'So what's up with you?' he said, staring at me. 'What's made you so flipping miserable?'

I turned away and stared out of the window. 'Nothing really,' I lied.

'Come off it,' he insisted. 'You wouldn't be bunking off school unless you had a good reason.'

And so, although I shall never know why, I told him.

6

James didn't say anything for a minute or two. Then he said, 'Got any money? I only had enough for the Cokes.'

I shrugged. Hadn't he heard a word I'd said? 'A few quid,' I told him.

'Right.' He got up and grabbed my hand. 'Come on, let's get out of here.'

He dragged me along to the bus stop. I had to run to keep up with him. By the time we got there, I was out of breath and still wondering why he hadn't said anything about what I'd said. I still couldn't believe I'd actually told him.

'Have you gone bonkers?' I panted.

'Nope.' He leaned out into the road to see if there was anything coming. Amongst the herd of traffic heading our way I could see a cream and green single decker crawling towards us. 'I thought we'd take a trip,' he added.

'Where?'

The moon? Saturn? A galaxy far away?

'The beach,' he said. Then he added as the bus got nearer, 'Great, it's the right one.'

I hung back. 'James, you're barmy. What will we do at the beach? It's freezing cold and bleak as Siberia down there.'

'No, it's not,' he said as the bus hissed to a halt beside us. 'Get your dosh out.'

Like a dummy I fished in my pocket and found a fiver.

'Two returns to Stoneness please, mate,' James said to the driver, holding his hand out for *my* money.

He got the tickets and we stumbled to the back of the bus and plonked down on the seat.

'There you are.' He leaned back, stretched out his legs and put his hands behind his head. 'Easy.'

I stared out of the window as we cruised along the High Street and past the school. I thought of all the kids in there bent over their desks or in the gym or art room. That's just what they were—kids. '*You're only sixteen,*' my mum had said but suddenly I felt as if I was as old as history.

The houses thinned and we were heading towards the coast. I could see the sun peeping out between the hills like an eye staring at us. I looked at James out of the corner of my vision. He was staring into space, a far-away look on his face. He *still* hadn't said anything about what I'd told him. I began to wonder if he'd even *heard*.

'James,' I said. 'Why are we doing this?'

He turned his head and grinned. 'It's just what we need,' he said. 'A walk along the beach. It helps you get your brain sorted. Haven't you ever tried it?'

I shrugged. 'Nope.'

If I want to think about stuff I usually listen to my CDs, stare out of the window at the sky or get lost in some fantasy book or other. Things like that usually help but it hadn't worked lately. Nothing had and I'd begun to wonder if anything ever would again.

'I come whenever I can,' James was saying dreamily. 'Just me and the waves and sky and the seagulls.' He turned to me. 'It works. It really does.' He tapped his forehead. 'Gets the old brainbox sorted.'

I almost said I didn't know he had one but stopped myself just in time. It would have been an awful thing to say anyway. James *did* have a brain, much more of a brain than anyone had ever given him credit for. It was just that behaving like an animal had kept it a secret all these years. It looked as if we both were pretty good at keeping secrets.

We got off the bus and just stood there breathing in the fresh air. The shore was deserted and bleak in the keen autumn wind. Brown and withered leaves blew about inside the bus shelter like little messages reminding us that summer was a dream away.

James must have seen me shiver.

'Come on,' he said. 'It'll be sheltered under the wall.'

We walked down the steps and on to the pebbles. I loved the noise our shoes made as we crunched along. It sounded as if we were walking on a carpet of broken biscuits. The tide was way, way out, a shining ribbon at the end of an endless landscape of sand and mud. It had left pools of gleaming water stretching so far you could hardly make out where the sea broke over the land. A little flock of waders scurried up and down, their sharp beaks bobbing in and out as they went.

The beach curved in a wide arc and in the distance you could see the looming outline of the power station. A few fishing boats were moored high up on the bank of pebbles. Their masts clanked in the wind.

James had stopped and was standing still and taking deep breaths of air and staring out to the horizon.

'Cool, isn't it?' he said, his eyes shining. He gazed out to sea as if he might see a great ship coming to take us away. 'This is what I want one day,' he said, brushing the hair out of his eyes.

'What?' I asked.

'To live near the sea,' he went on. 'So I can wake every morning and see and smell and feel the ocean. Magic.'

'Yes, it would be fantastic,' I said. James was full of surprises. I would never have thought someone like him cared about that kind of thing.

'When I was little,' he went on. 'We used to go to a place on the west coast for our holidays. That's before my old man started drinking. It was great. Not cold and bleak like this. The town was brilliant. There was a funfair and arcades, a pier where you could walk right out into the sea and look back and see the whole town spread out . . . ' he paused for breath. The picture he painted was so vivid I could really see it.

'Do you reckon you'll ever get to live there?' I asked.

He shrugged. 'Doubt it. Unless I win the lottery.' His eyes shone. 'If I did then I'd take Mum and the kids with me.'

'Sometimes if you want something hard enough you make it come true,' I said almost believing myself.

He turned to me, the wind making tears in his eyes. 'Yeah? Who's been telling you fairy stories?'

I didn't say anything else. The truth was I didn't know *what* to say. This wasn't the boy I knew, the one who behaved like a moron most of the time. This was someone else. Someone with hopes and dreams just like I used to have.

So instead I simply took a deep breath of air too. James was right. It *was* great here. I had a sudden urge to run. Run so fast along the sand I turned into a blur and fell off the edge of the world.

'Race you.' I flung him a grin then dashed off down towards the sand. My coat flapped behind me like wings and my bag banged heavily against my side. I didn't care that I was getting my trousers soaked, my shoes coated in wet sand. It was just great to be running like that. Free as a bird. I could feel the sea-wind on my face, the salt tang of the air against my lips and in my ears.

James caught me up in no time. Laughing, red in the face, he sped past.

'Pig,' I yelled.

When he reached the edge of the water he stopped and waited. Flushed, hair all over the place. His eyes glowed. I was out of breath, panting so much that I bent over with my hands on my knees.

He was looking at me, grinning. 'Feel better?'

I had to admit that I did even if my heart was beating so painfully I thought it might jump out of my chest and my lungs ached like billy-o.

We strolled along slowly after that. Under our feet, the hard ridges of the sand left by the receding tide felt just like cobblestones. Now and then James bent to pick up a shell or pull a bit of seaweed from its burial place in the sand.

'You can tell what the weather is by this,' he said, holding a long piece of weed up to the breeze.

'You can tell what the weather's like by looking out of the window,' I said scornfully.

He chuckled and tossed it at me. It curled round my neck like a slimy snake. I tore at it then flung it down on the sand, laughing and calling him names.

'So,' he said when he could get a word in, 'what are you going to do?'

I sobered up as it all came crashing back to me. The thing I was trying to forget. There was no pretending I didn't know what he meant.

'Have the operation, I suppose,' I said.

'You don't have to if you don't want to.' James didn't look at me, just at the place miles ahead where the cliff sliced the beach in two.

'I know,' I said. 'But I do want to. I'm just scared out my brain that's all.'

'You're sure, are you?' he said, looking at me as if he could see right into my head.

I frowned. 'What do you mean?'

'I mean, you're sure that's what you want . . . an abortion?'

And when I looked at him I knew that he was the only person who *could* see right into my head. He could even see it better than I could.

When I burst into tears he stopped and put his arms round me. I guess that's what I'd wanted all along. Someone to put their arms around me and hold me tight. Hold me so I felt safe like that little Derwent kid

I'd held in the restaurant. I felt strange. As if everything that was happening to me was somehow tied up with the Derwent family and again everything was spinning out of control and I was helpless to stop it.

We just stood there for a minute. Two people together on the edge of the ocean. Eventually I pulled away, feeling a wally.

'Sorry,' I sniffed and wiped my nose on my sleeve. 'I'm being a total wimp, aren't I?'

He didn't say anything which probably meant he agreed with me. He just waited while I sniffed again and stared out at the horizon for a minute or two. Then he took my arm and said, 'Come on, let's walk.'

We talked for ages after that. Walking and talking. Arm in arm like a couple of old crumblies.

I told him everything. How I'd been flattered by Steve at the party. How stupid I felt. How I'd let everyone down and getting an abortion was the only way I could make it up to them. How I knew it was the best and most sensible thing to do even though I just couldn't get my head round it and I was more scared and guilty than I'd ever been in my life.

James shook his head. 'You shouldn't have it done if you're not sure,' he said, meaning the abortion. 'It's your body. You can do what you like with it.'

But I shook my head, still crying an ocean into the grimy hanky he'd dragged from his pocket and handed to me without a word. Surely someone like him should know better than anyone that you can't always do everything you want.

'It's not that I *really* want to have a baby,' I sobbed, barely able to put my feelings into words. 'I just don't want to kill it, that's all.'

'Kill it?' he said. 'It's not really even a—'

'I know,' I broke in. 'But it still feels as if it'll be murder.'

He shook his head. 'It won't be, honestly it won't.'

'It'll still feel like it,' I insisted.

He gazed at me. 'Then don't have it done,' he said as if it was the easiest thing in the world. 'Really,' he insisted. 'I mean it. Don't have it done.'

I sobbed. 'It's not that simple.'

He put his hand on my shoulder. 'No, I suppose not.'

I shook my head. 'If I don't it'll ruin everything.'

'Who for?' he said.

'My parents,' I sniffed.

'It's your kid, not theirs.'

'I know but I can't separate myself from them.'

'Why not?'

I shrugged. 'I just can't. I'm not old enough, I suppose. Not ready.'

'I reckon they'll stick by you, whatever you decide.'

I shook my head sorrowfully. 'Will they?'

My trainers sloshed in the sand as we walked along. Blobs of it splashed up James's tracksuit bottoms. He didn't seem to notice. Looking at me, his hand still on my shoulder, all he seemed to notice was how sad I was. Sadder than ever I'd been in my life. Although I hated to admit it, the thing I had been desperately trying to avoid all along had happened. The zygote had become a baby in my head.

I knew then that in spite of what I did or didn't want I had to have the operation soon before I changed my mind and mucked up my dreams for ever.

7

'Don't forget,' James said when we got back to town, 'you do whatever you want.'

He didn't seem to understand that what I wanted wasn't really relevant.

'OK,' I said. 'Thanks, James. I hope you don't get into trouble for bunking off.'

'Me too,' he said, pulling a face.

I put my arms round him and hugged him and didn't care if the world saw.

When I pulled away I saw he'd gone red again. 'What's that for?' he muttered.

'For helping me.'

He shrugged. 'I haven't done anything.'

'Yes, you have.' And before he could answer I hugged him again then turned and headed for home. On the corner I spun round to wave but he had gone.

When I got there Mum was in the front room sorting out her books and files for college.

'Where have you been?' she asked as soon as I got through the door. It was no good lying so all I could do was shrug.

'I couldn't face school.'

'You should have said,' she went on angrily. 'It would have saved me the embarrassment of lying when they phoned up to find out where you were.'

My hair made a veil across my cheek as I hung my head. I couldn't do anything right. I just mumbled *sorry* and ran upstairs to fling myself on the bed. I felt as if I was going crazy, or the

61

whole world was crazy and I was the only sane one in it.

She came up later with a cup of tea.

'I'm sorry, Cass,' she said when it should have been me who was apologizing. 'I know you're going through a rotten time but you'll feel OK when it's all over. And you'll understand it's for the best.'

I sniffed. 'Will I?'

She moved towards me and I thought for a minute she was going to hug me but she didn't. She just straightened the duvet where I'd crumpled it all up. 'Yes,' she said. 'Of course you will. This time next year you'll have forgotten all about it.'

'Will I?' I repeated like some crazy parrot.

She sighed. 'Yes. Cass, you've got so much to look forward to . . . all those things that I didn't get the chance to do.' She sat down, fiddling with her wedding ring, turning it round and round as if it was a screw that kept her finger on. 'Cass . . . ' She said it in such a way that I got a feeling something momentous was about to happen. That she was going to tell me some big secret that she'd never told anyone before in her life.

I was right, she was.

'Your dad and me had to get married,' she said.

'*Had* to?' I said. 'You mean you were . . . ?'

'Yes,' she said. 'I was pregnant.'

'Oh, blimey.' I didn't know what else to say. Or what she *wanted* me to say.

'So you see I never got the chance to do lots of things I wanted to do,' she said. 'I *know* what it's like to have your dreams ruined.'

'You weren't sorry, though, were you?' An icy blast seemed to be blowing over my skin. Supposing she blamed me for all her shattered dreams? 'You didn't—?'

She shook her head and smiled sadly. 'No, Cass, I'm not sorry I married your dad. We'd been going out together for ages. And you know I'm not sorry I had you. But it's not what I want for you, Cass. I want you

62

to experience all those wonderful things I didn't get the chance to.'

'What things did you want to do?' I asked, curious to know exactly what she'd given up.

'Travel for one thing . . . ' She got up and went over to the window, staring out. 'Like your gran. You can't imagine how envious I used to be of her.'

'You've been abroad,' I said stupidly not understanding; at least not wanting to admit to myself that I was suddenly beginning to understand my mum better than I understood myself.

She shrugged. 'For holidays, yes, but that's not really travelling. Seeing the real countries. You don't get much idea of what a place is like when you're stuck round a hotel swimming pool with a small child.'

'Did you hate it, then?' I asked.

She turned swiftly. 'No, of course not. We had some great times. I just wish I'd done more things before I got tied down, that's all.'

'You could have sent me to a childminder,' I said.

She shook her head. 'No, I believed that if you had a child you should be the one to look after it.' She shrugged. 'I was lucky. Your dad earned enough so I didn't have to go out to work.'

'Millions of kids do go to childminders,' I argued. 'It doesn't do them any harm.'

'I know,' Mum said. 'And I'm sure that's fine for them. It just wasn't how I wanted to live my life, that's all.'

I managed a grin. 'Well, you can do all the things you want to do when you're old, like Gran.'

She sighed, then smiled. 'Before then, I hope.'

She came back to sit on the bed with a funny half-smile on her face. She reached out for my hand. When she found it she held it tight even though I tried to pull away.

'Don't miss the chance, Cass, don't tie yourself down. There will be another time for you to have a child . . . the *right* time.'

I swallowed. 'It just seems such a terrible thing to do.'

She shook her head. 'Having an unwanted child is a terrible thing to do.'

'It wouldn't be unwanted. Not by me. Not if I decided not to go through with the abortion. It would mean I *did* want it.'

There . . . I'd said it at last. The whole truth and nothing but the truth. I couldn't explain it, even to myself. I *knew* what it would be like, having a kid at my age. I *knew* it would spoil my dreams.

I half expected her to explode but she didn't. She just gave me another funny, sad half-smile. 'You're just romanticizing it, Cass. You'd want it at first. Tiny, dependent babies are wonderful. But later, when you realized all the things you wouldn't be able to do because of it.'

'I'm not stupid, Mum,' I said.

Then she said something else. Something that freaked my mind out again. I felt I was on a roller-coaster, up one minute then plunging down the next.

'Cass, whatever happens . . . we'll stick by you, you know.'

Her eyes were bright with tears as she looked at me and I knew suddenly that in spite of what she said she wouldn't stop me having the baby if that's what I really wanted. Even if it did mean us both having a bucketful of shattered dreams. James had been right. They would stand by me . . . whatever happened. But I could see by Mum's face that she was scared. Really scared I'd put my foot down and refuse to have the operation. Scared how it would affect her life and Dad's . . . and mine.

'Thanks,' I croaked, not really knowing what else to say. I knew how hard it was for her to have said that.

She patted my leg and let go of my hand. I desperately wanted to say '*It's OK, Mum, you needn't worry,*' but I couldn't, not just then. Saying it would mean I'd finally made up my mind and that wouldn't have been true. Not yet . . . not quite yet.

I dreaded going to school the following day but Mum insisted I went. She even took me in her car to make sure that's where I was really going when I left the house. She dropped me off at the school gates on her way to college. I was still in a foul mood and slammed out of the car without even saying goodbye.

I dawdled up the drive reluctantly. I really dreaded James telling people we'd spent the day together. My friends probably wouldn't believe him but his mates, or his old mates if he'd been telling me the truth, would never let me forget it.

When I got to school there was a police car outside and some kind of hoo-ha going on in the Head's office.

Mel was waiting for me by the gym.

She linked her arm through mine. 'Were you ill yesterday?'

I shook my head.

'Bunking off?'

'I just couldn't face it,' I told her.

'How're your parents?'

'Sick,' I said.

'Are you dreading tomorrow?' I'd already told her when my appointment was.

'Yes,' I told her. 'Please . . . don't remind me.'

'Is your mum going with you?'

'No, I'm going by myself.'

She looked horrified. 'You can't do that,' she protested. 'I'll come with you.'

I shook my head. 'It's OK, honestly.'

How could I tell her that my head was like a closed door with me inside just wanting to be on my own to sort things out. No one had the key . . . at least I didn't think they had until I met James. Even though she was my best friend I don't think she would have understood.

There were a couple of policemen walking down the corridor towards us. They had some people with them: James and two others. They all looked pretty grim. I stared at them in horror and James gave me a sideways look as they went past, out of the main doors. I saw them go down the drive and get into the police car.

Mel saw me staring. 'Hadn't you heard?'

'Heard what?'

'Some old woman was mugged in the shopping mall yesterday lunchtime and she said it was a bunch of boys from here.'

'What's that got to do with James and the others?'

Mel shrugged. 'Well, it's bound to be them, isn't it.'

That annoyed me. It was stupid to jump to conclusions like that. Then I realized that a few days ago I would probably have done exactly the same.

'Not necessarily,' I protested then hurriedly racked my brain for something else to say before she got suspicious. 'I mean, it could have been anybody.'

She snorted. 'Yeah, well, they all bunked off yesterday so what do you think?'

I shrugged and shut my mouth before I really put my foot in it. 'I don't know,' I fibbed. I tried to put James to the back of my mind but somehow I couldn't. I kept thinking about him protesting his innocence at the police station and no one believing him. I wondered if he would tell them he'd been with me and they would ask me if he was telling the truth. But when no one did I decided he hadn't.

When the last bell went and I still hadn't seen James I headed home simply not knowing what to do. Maybe I should go down to the police station and declare I'd got an alibi for James? Then I thought I'd look a real twit if they'd let him go anyway. A feeling of doom and destruction settled in my stomach. Even though I knew the old woman couldn't identify him because he definitely hadn't been there. The trouble is you could never be sure. You'd only got to watch *The Bill* to know people got wrongly identified every day.

Poor James.

Poor me . . . poor everybody.

The house was empty when I got in. I'm about the

only person I know whose Mum is almost always there when they get home from school. Mel's mum works long shifts and is hardly ever there at all. She'd got her own tea and stuff since she was about ten.

There was a letter addressed to me on the kitchen table. When I opened it, it was the result of my blood test. I wasn't HIV positive. I was really relieved even though I'd never really let myself think that I might be. It wasn't that I didn't know it could have been a *real* possibility. After all, you can't tell just by looking at someone whether they're going to infect you or not. It was just that I'd put it into that little corner of my brain where I store all the things I'm too scared to think about. Like death and disease and failing my exams and getting pregnant.

I left the letter on the table for Mum to see. At least that would be one thing she wouldn't have to worry about.

I mooched around in the kitchen for a while, drinking half a can of Coke then not fancying the rest. Watching a bit of TV then flicking through a magazine or two. Mum had left instructions for putting the dinner on. Not that I didn't know how to. I guess she just didn't trust me to remember. She imagined I'd go off to my room and read or do my homework and forget all about it. Which I probably would have done.

I was sitting in the front room, staring at the TV screen and thinking about James and still wondering what I should do when I heard Mum's car in the drive.

She was wearing jeans and a black sweater and had her arms full of files and books. She dumped them on the floor and fell into a chair with a sigh.

'What a brilliant day!' she said although I hadn't asked. Her eyes shone. 'Two great lectures and . . . ' She took a file out of her bag. 'I got B plus for my first essay, not bad, huh?'

I hadn't even realized she'd been writing her first essay.

She put the file back in her bag, not even noticing I didn't comment. 'Right, did you put the dinner on?'

My hand flew to my mouth. 'No, I forgot.' Then I mumbled, 'Sorry.'

She was going to shout at me but stopped herself just in time. I was glad. The mood I was in I would have screamed blue murder if she yelled at me.

Instead she just slammed her lips tight together. 'Well, we'll just have to have a late dinner whether your dad likes it or not.' She used to talk about being proud to always have the dinner ready when he got home. I guessed those days were gone.

I followed her into the kitchen as she bustled about getting stuff ready. She rattled on about the other students . . . about what a mixed bunch they were . . . the things they'd been studying, stuff about Freud and Nature versus Nurture and Child Development and things like that. I sat on a kitchen stool only half hearing what she was on about. One thing I couldn't help noticing though was how happy she looked. Her pleasure radiated from her like a sunny day. She didn't notice me staring at her with a mind like a whirlpool, round and round . . . a turmoil of regret and sorrow and guilt.

Then she noticed the letter. She picked it up, scanned it rapidly, sighed, then put it down again. 'Well,' she said. 'That's one less thing to worry about.'

I didn't answer.

Then she began peeling the spuds to make chips, all the time nattering on about college. She seemed to take on a new life . . . a new energy. She wasn't even going to be a slave to her family any more, she was saying. They were all old enough to fend for themselves.

She turned suddenly and smiled at me. 'Cass, I think this is going to be the best time of my life.'

Then, staring at me, she suddenly put down the knife and came towards me. 'Oh, Cass, I'm sorry . . . you're feeling so miserable, the last thing you want to hear is what a great time I'm having . . . and I'm really pleased your blood test was OK . . . I . . . '

'So'm I and it's OK,' I said quickly. 'I'm glad college is going to be good.' I hoped she couldn't tell I didn't mean it. I hated her being so happy. Why couldn't I feel like that too?

I got down off the stool before she reached me. I was frightened that if she touched me I would cry and never stop.

'I'm just going to do my homework,' I muttered.

'Did you hand in the note?' She meant the one about me having the next day off.

'Yeah.' I'd handed it to my form teacher.

'Did she say anything?'

'No.' I was heading for the door.

She held my arm as I went past. 'Cass, for God's sake talk to me.'

'I am talking to you.'

'You're not, you're just mumbling at me.'

I shrugged. 'I'm sorry.' The last thing I wanted was a row although it looked as if we were just about to have one.

'Cass . . . ' She had her face close to mine. 'You must let me come with you tomorrow.'

'No,' I said quickly. 'I want to go by myself.'

'Cass, you can't!'

'I can. For God's sake leave me alone!' I knew I was yelling at her but I couldn't help it. She flinched as she looked at my red, angry face. Was this the little girl she had known only a few weeks ago? Her sweet little Cass, the apple of her dad's eye. I knew I was still wounding her . . . I simply couldn't help it.

'But they'll think it's terrible,' she went on. 'A sixteen-year-old all on her own. They'll think you haven't got a mother or father, or anyone to help you.'

'I don't care what they think. And I don't *need* any help!' I was still yelling at her.

'Well, I care.' She was shouting back now. 'And I'm coming, Cass, whether you like it or not.'

I stared at her, eyes blazing into hers. Suddenly I sagged. Defeated. 'OK.' I was suddenly too tired and too fed up to argue. 'Do what you want.'

And anyway, in the long run it didn't make any difference.

I'd finally made up my mind what I was going to do.

PART TWO

8

The next time I really spoke to James was after Christmas. I'd seen him at school, of course, mooching around the corridors, standing on his own in the playground. I'd tried to talk to him but he didn't seem to want to know, turning away whenever I went near. I wanted to find out what had happened about that mugging incident. I asked around but no one seemed to know, or care, what the outcome had been. And I suppose I'd still been too tied up in my own selfish misery to make much of an effort to find out for myself.

It was the spring half-term when I came across him. I'd decided to go for a walk in the park. Things still weren't great at home. Christmas had been a nightmare, New Year even worse. Everyone was losing patience with me. Mum. Dad . . . even Mel. I knew it was about time I snapped out of it.

'You should really be feeling your old self again by now, Cass,' Mum had said that morning. 'Time heals everything, you know.'

'Does it?' I'd looked up from the book I was reading at the breakfast table.

She stood with her back to the sink. 'Yes, Cass. It has to. We can't grieve for things for ever.'

I shut the book with a bang. 'No,' I said. 'I suppose not.'

It was then I decided to go out for a walk. The truth was, I *had* begun to feel better. For some strange reason, though, I didn't want her to know. I suppose I was still punishing her . . . me . . . everyone. Maybe I was being a martyr. All those feelings of guilt and sorrow and pain had been taken over by a sense of relief. And I knew I'd done the right thing. I was still sad, of course. I didn't think I could ever be as sad about anything again for the rest of my life. And I still hated myself for being so stupid. I thought I'd always feel like that. But I knew I'd never be my old self again. That Cass had gone, disappeared for ever. Maybe *that's* what I was grieving for now. My childhood.

I was walking by the lake when I came across James. It was one of those bright days when the air crackles with frost and everything sparkles like new.

I didn't actually notice him until I almost tripped over him. I'd been off on another planet as usual. Spacewalking in my own universe.

'Cass!'

His voice brought me down to earth.

I looked down and there he was sitting on the damp grass, staring up at me. He had an old tatty sports bag beside him, stuffed full of something. He looked so cold and miserable I felt a horrible pang of guilt. Good old Cass, I thought to myself, so tied up with your own problems you'd only given a fleeting thought to his.

'Hi, James.' I sat down beside him and hugged my knees. I didn't care if I caught one of those things your mum always tells you you'll catch if you sit on damp grass.

'You all right?' James asked.

'I'm OK,' I said. When I turned to look at him I noticed he looked absolutely terrible. His hair was a mess, he hadn't shaved, and his clothes were crumpled and grubby. Worse still he had a bruise on the side of his face as big as an apple.

I stared at him. 'God,' I said. 'What happened to you, James?'

'Fell off my bike,' he said although I'd got a sneaky feeling he wasn't telling the truth. As far as I knew he didn't even have a bike.

'You still training for that sponsored run?' I asked stupidly. It was obvious James wasn't training for anything but despair.

'No,' he said. 'Given up.'

'Why?' I asked.

He shrugged and stared out across to the deserted kids' play area opposite the lake. 'Dunno,' he said. 'I just got fed up.'

I bit my lip. It was a real shame. Running had been doing him good. 'What about the little kid who was sick?' I asked.

He shrugged again. 'No idea.'

I went on staring at him. He didn't only look terrible, he sounded terrible as well. Talking in a deadpan voice as if he didn't care about anyone or anything.

He picked a blade of grass and stuck it between his two front teeth. 'How are you now, anyway?' he said.

It was my turn to shrug. 'I'm OK.'

'You had it done, didn't you?'

I supposed it was obvious I wasn't pregnant, it would have begun to show by now.

'Yes,' I said and for a moment the scenery blurred.

'I'm sorry,' he said.

'So am I,' I said. 'Not sorry I had it done. Just sorry I was stupid enough to let it happen in the first place.'

We sat in silence for a minute or two. The memory of my time in hospital came crashing back. It had hardly even been twenty-four hours. In one morning, out early the next. The nurses had been kind, giving me pills for my pain and tissues for my tears. I'd gone to Doctor Janet for a check up a day or so later and she'd offered me more counselling.

'No thanks,' I'd said.

'But it could help you, Cass,' she'd told me. 'Counselling helps all kinds of people. Alcoholics, people who've suffered violence, people with serious emotional problems. Please, Cass.'

But I'd still said no. I hadn't wanted to talk about it

75

any more. All I'd wanted to do was lock it away. There hadn't even been any scars to remind me. Not on my skin, anyway.

'Did they *make* you?' James was asking.

I shook my head. 'No. Actually, everyone was brilliant.'

I told him about the counsellor I'd seen at the hospital, before I'd had the operation.

'She was great,' I said. 'She explained all about what would happen and asked me how I felt about it.'

'What did you tell her?' James was staring at me.

I shrugged again. 'Nothing much. I felt so awful I couldn't find the right words to describe how I felt. But I think she knew that.'

'Poor old Cass,' James said.

I managed a grin. 'Yeah. I suppose it helped though, talking to someone who understood.' I gazed at him. 'They're good, those people. They don't criticize you or anything. I suppose they're used to hearing about all the awful things that happen to people.'

'Yeah,' James said.

I was just about to say something else when he suddenly jumped to his feet.

'Got to go,' he mumbled. He began hurrying away, so fast it didn't dawn on me for a minute that he was actually leaving.

I jumped up too.

'James,' I shouted. 'Wait! I wanted to ask you something.'

He waited. 'What?'

'I wanted to know about that mugging last term. When I've tried to talk to you about it, you've avoided me.'

'Have I?' he muttered. 'Sorry.'

'Well?' I said. 'What happened?'

'Oh, the old woman decided it wasn't me after all.'

'That's good,' I said. 'You know I would have stood up for you . . . told them you were with me.'

He shrugged. 'Yeah, well, you didn't have to, did you.'

He sounded so fed up that I put my hand on his arm. 'James, what's wrong?'

He pulled a face. 'My old man never did believe I wasn't involved,' he said. 'He almost killed me when he heard about it. Trashed my stuff and everything looking for things she'd had pinched.'

'But that's crazy! She said you weren't—'

'I know,' James interrupted. 'He's always looking for an excuse to take things out on me.'

I was horrified. I *knew* James hadn't really fallen off a bike. 'What things?'

'I dunno,' James said. 'Anything he feels mad about.' His face closed up. 'God, I hate that bloke.'

'Doesn't your mum do anything about it?' I asked 'Doesn't she try to stop him hitting you?'

He shrugged. 'What can she do? She's scared stiff of him anyway. If she interferes she gets it too.'

'Oh, James.' I was so horrified I couldn't think of anything else to say.

'Yeah,' he said bitterly. 'Gross, isn't it?'

We were through the gates by now and out on to the main road.

'Well,' he said awkwardly. He didn't seem to be able to look me in the eye. 'See ya, then, Cass.'

'But, James—' I started to say but he'd already gone. Walking away, head down, feet scuffing the pavement, in the direction of the railway station. As I watched he hitched the sports bag up over his shoulder, turned into Station Road and disappeared from sight. I felt helpless and hopeless. I wanted to run after him, help him like he'd helped me but somehow he'd put up a wall round himself. Exactly as I had done. I understood how he felt, just wanting to shrink into himself and disappear. I'd felt like that for so long it had got to be a habit. Worse still, there had been lots of things I wanted to say to him. Thanks again for being with me on the beach that day . . . thanks for listening. It had really helped. I guessed I'd just have to say those things another time.

Mum was studying in the front room when I got back. I was already halfway up to my room when she emerged.

'Had a nice walk?'

'Yes, thanks.'

'What are you going to do now?'

I knew she was concerned about me but I wished she'd just leave me alone.

So I shrugged and said 'nothing' and went on up to my room. I could feel her eyes following me. Being horrible was getting to be a habit I couldn't get out of. Maybe they'd be better off without me.

I went to the park the following day, hoping I'd see James again. But he wasn't there. I went again the next, then walked into town to see if he was hanging around the shopping mall. I looked in the arcade where his old mates spent most of their time but he wasn't with them. I phoned Mel and asked her if she'd spotted him around town.

'James Derwent?' she burst out. 'That idiot. What on earth do you want to see him for?'

'Oh, nothing really,' I fibbed. 'I just wondered if you'd seen him, that's all.'

Mel made a sound as if she thought I was off my trolley then went on to tell me about a club she'd been to with Michael. I tried to sound interested but all the time my mind was wandering back to James and the way he'd been when I met him in the park.

When Mel had rung off I got the book and looked up his number. But he didn't seem to have a phone.

Finally, I decided to go round to his house. I kept asking myself why but I couldn't come up with a decent answer. Only that I'd spent the last forty-eight hours thinking about someone else other than myself so that seemed as good a reason as any. The knowledge that things were so terribly wrong kept crashing in on me. I still hadn't forgotten how James had listened to my problems. Now maybe it was time I listened to his.

The estate where James lived had got worse since I'd been there before. Going there was like landing on another planet.

It must have been dustbin day because the pavements were littered with black sacks. Lots had been scavenged by cats and dogs and stuff was scattered all over the place. Bits of food, milk cartons, dirty nappies. In the square a gang of kids were playing suicide games jumping off the graffitied walls and kicking a ball around. I recognized one of them. James's brother. One who went to our school.

'Hey, Ricky,' I called. 'Is James in?'

His mates stared at me as if I was an alien as he left them and came over. 'What?' he squinted at me through short-sighted eyes. James had told me he needed to wear glasses but his mum couldn't afford to get any.

'I said is James in?'

'No, he's scarpered.' Ricky scratched at the eczema on the back of his hands.

'What do you mean?' I felt my stomach lurch, a hard tight lump of fear knotted itself inside me.

'He's gone, 'opped it,' Ricky said. 'Run away.'

I closed my eyes for a minute hoping that when I opened them I'd gone back in time and Ricky was just about to say, '*Yeah, he's in.*' But when I did open them Ricky was still there in front of me, chewing gum and scratching and jiggling his football about in his hands.

'What do you mean?' I asked again as if I was some thicko that couldn't understand English.

'What I say,' Ricky said. 'He run away on Monday. Mum's going spare.'

Monday . . . that was the day I saw him in the park. 'Where's he gone?' I asked stupidly.

Ricky shrugged. 'Dunno, no one knows.' Then one of his mates came and punched the ball out of his hand.

Ricky swore and ran after him leaving me standing there like a dummy, my mind frozen as an iceberg.

When I came to I headed for his house. I *had* to talk to his mum. Find out what had happened and if she had any idea at all where James had gone.

James's front path was littered with broken plastic toys, bits of wood, cardboard boxes. The skeleton cars were still there.

I wheeled my bike through the mess and parked it by the front door. Inside, I could hear someone shouting. I knocked loudly.

A child of about six opened it. A girl with dark rat-tailed hair. She screwed up her nose and leaned the side of her face against the door.

'Is your mum in?' I asked.

She didn't answer. Instead she turned and yelled, 'Mum, a girl's here.'

Mrs Derwent appeared. 'Yes?' she said, peering at me as if she recognized me but couldn't think where she'd seen me before. Her eyes were red rimmed. I could tell she'd been crying.

'I'm a friend of James's—' I began.

'Oh yes, I've seen you before. You don't know where he is, do you?' she asked quickly before I could comment.

I shook my head. 'No, I'm sorry, I wish I did. Er . . . I saw Ricky . . . has James really run away?'

'Yes.' I could see she was fighting back tears. 'I'll kill him when he comes back, scaring us like this.'

'He told me he'd been rowing with his dad,' I said.

'Rowing?' Mrs Derwent said. 'Fighting, you mean.'

'Well,' I said. 'Whatever.'

Behind her, another child began to cry and someone turned the TV up loud so they could hear above it. 'You'd better come in,' Mrs Derwent said and so I stepped through the front door into the house from hell.

'Come into the kitchen,' she said. 'I was just making a cup of tea.' I followed her through. She took a pile of

80

dirty washing off a chair and asked me to sit down. The table was littered with the remains of breakfast and probably dinner too. There was an old-fashioned dresser in one corner piled up with newspapers and rubbish. On one shelf was a picture of James taken in his tracksuit when it was new. He'd told me he earned the money for it doing a paper round until his so-called mates had persuaded him only wimps did paper rounds and he'd packed it in.

'My name's Cass.' I tried not to look at the remains of someone's porridge. 'I met you in McDonald's a little while ago. I'm in James's class at school.'

'Yes, I remember.' She bustled about, rinsing two dirty mugs under the tap and putting tea bags in them. 'Sugar?'

'No thanks.' I grasped the grimy mug as she handed it to me. She quickly cleared a space, ramming dirty dishes and cutlery into an already full sink. Then she sat down too.

She gazed at me. 'You haven't got any idea where James might have gone, have you? I'm so worried about him.'

I shook my head, feeling guilty because that day I should have guessed. The stuffed sports bag, his mood, I *knew* something was desperately wrong but I hadn't done anything about it. Typical of waste-of-space me.

'No idea,' I said. 'Have you told the police?'

'Bill phoned them,' she said. I guessed Bill was James's dad. 'They took details but said he hadn't been gone long enough for them to get really worried.'

'Are you sure he's actually run away?' I swallowed and the words would hardly come out. 'Maybe he's gone to stay with one of his mates?'

She got up wearily from the kitchen table and took a piece of paper down off the shelf above the fridge. It was a note from James.

'I found it in under my pillow,' she said.

Sorry, Mum, it said. *I just can't stand him any longer. I'll get in touch as soon as I can.*

'He means his dad?' I gazed at her and saw she was crying. She nodded speechlessly. I didn't know what to say. Words like a lump of that porridge in the bowl seemed to be stuck in my throat. I wanted to tell her I understood what it was like to lose someone who had grown inside you but the words just wouldn't come out.

'They've never got on,' James's mum sniffed. 'They're too much alike, I suppose. Both got tempers. He's really upset Jamie's gone. He feels guilty.' She sighed. 'He always feels guilty when it's too late.'

'Yes, well, he should,' I blurted out before I could stop myself.

Mrs Derwent wiped her face on her sleeve. 'I'm so scared that something will happen to Jamie. I've seen programmes about youngsters on the streets, it's terrible. Everyone thinks he's tough but he isn't really.'

'No,' I said. 'I know he isn't.'

Mrs Derwent sighed and wiped her hand across her eyes.

I looked down at my hands. 'I'm sorry,' I said lamely.

She stared into her cup as if she might find the answers to her problems in there.

I leaned forward. 'Are you sure you haven't got any idea where he might have gone?'

She shook her head. 'No, none. I've got a sister up north who he's quite fond of but I phoned her and he's not there. She promised to let me know if he turned up.'

In the other room, two of the kids were fighting over the TV. 'Belt up, you two!' Mrs Derwent yelled and when they didn't she stormed down the hall to sort them out. I got up and took down the photo of James. It was before he'd lost weight and had his hair cut but it was still a good likeness. I stared at it for a second or two then, although I didn't really know why, I stuffed it into the inside pocket of my jacket.

I racked my brains for ideas about where he might

have gone. Then, as Mrs Derwent came back into the kitchen, I remembered something—the town he'd gone to on holiday when he was a kid. Dartcombe it was called. My stomach turned over. I bet that's where he was. I bet he'd gone there searching for his dream.

An idea was sprouting in my head as I finished my tea. I got out my note book and wrote down my phone number. 'Will you let me know if he comes back?' I ripped out the page.

'Yes.' She took the bit of paper and stuck it on the dresser with all the other junk.

As I got up to go, the front door banged and we heard footsteps coming towards the kitchen. Mrs Derwent leapt up and started running the tap over the dirty dishes. A man came into the room. I could tell it was James's dad. He had the same dark hair and eyes although he was short and slight, hardly taller than me. He had a purple bruise just below one eye. At least James had got one punch in by the look of it.

He threw me a glance. 'Who's this?'

Close, I could smell he'd been to the pub.

'A friend of James's,' Mrs Derwent said without turning round.

James's dad stared at me. It was strange. After all I'd heard about him I thought he'd be a big man, a big bully with large hands and a large voice. He was small and weasely and didn't look as if he'd harm a fly. It just shows you can never tell what people are really like just by looking at them. Although I remembered afterwards that weasels are aggressive little creatures who can attack and kill something much bigger than themselves.

'What's your name, love?' he asked.

I told him.

'You in James's class?'

'Yes,' I said.

'You don't know where he's gone, I suppose?' he asked me.

I shook my head. 'No, I wish I did.'

'He's nothing but a waste of space, that kid.' Mr Derwent sat down with a sigh. 'Get us a beer, Chris.'

James's mum had said his dad felt guilty about him running away. Well, it didn't seem like it to me.

Mrs Derwent opened the fridge door. It was full of cans of beer and not much else. She got one and handed it to her husband without a word.

'W-well, I'd better get going,' I stuttered.

James's mum came to the door with me. 'You *will* let me know if you hear from him?'

'Yes,' I said. 'You too.'

'I will,' she said.

Dartcombe . . . the name spun around in my head as I rode home. West coast . . . I could go there, show people James's picture and ask if anyone had seen him. I knew I should have told his mum I suspected he might be there, but for some reason I wanted to keep it to myself. If I'd told her my suspicions then his dad might have gone shooting down there looking for him and James would have hated that. And hated *me* for putting them on to him.

By the time I reached my house I'd made my plans. If James *was* in Dartcombe and the place was as great as he'd described, who knows, I thought, I might even stay there with him. After all, last year, hadn't I wanted desperately to run away even though, at the time, there had been absolutely nowhere I could go?

9

When I got there though it wasn't a bit like I'd expected. James must have been remembering it through rose-coloured glasses. Lots of memories are like that. Especially ones we get when we're kids. Snowy Christmases, golden autumn days, sunny summers. They couldn't *all* have been great.

Mum hadn't been in when I got back from James's house. I knew if I'd told her where I was going she would have tried to stop me and it would only have led to a row. I didn't think I could stand another one. We'd had so many lately I was beginning to feel we would end up murdering one another if we didn't look out.

So I just left a note saying I was going away for a few days and they weren't to worry about me. I knew they *would* worry and I really hated upsetting them more than I had done already but this was just something I had to do. I stuffed some things into a bag. Clean pants, jeans, my trainers, shampoo, wash things. I took my dreamcatcher from its hook by the window. I touched the feathers, feeling their softness under my fingertips. I thought about the Native American women lovingly weaving them to put by their babies' cradles so their children would only have good dreams. Sadness began to creep over me, through my feet, my legs, stomach, head until my whole body was brimming. I swallowed back an ocean of tears and put the dreamcatcher into my bag. I didn't really know why. I suppose I wanted to take something with me that reminded me of home. In case I decided never to come back.

I'd taken all the money out of my piggy bank. It bought a ticket to Dartcombe with enough left over for a couple of nights in a bed and breakfast place if I needed it. I huddled on the platform hoping no one I knew would see me. The last thing I wanted was to have to explain to anybody where I was going.

When I got there it was windy and raining. Sharp needles driving into my face. I hadn't thought to bring my waterproof. James's vision of Dartcombe in the sun was the only one I'd had.

I stood outside the station like a lemon. Where did I begin? Everything looked so dismal and gloomy I began to regret coming already. In front of me a road stretched down to the sea. There were shops on either side, a dingy cinema, a bingo hall, a grey church spire from somewhere round the back. Could this really be the same place James had described that day we spent on the beach at Stoneness?

A few people scurried about under umbrellas. Across the road there was a café, *Josie's* it said above the steamed-up windows. It seemed as good a place as any to start.

It was full. Men, mostly. Sitting smoking fags, their hands clasped around huge mugs of steaming tea or tucking into egg and chips and taking drags of smoke in between mouthfuls. A couple of women in headscarves with shopping bags by their sides, sat next to an ancient juke box. Their faces were close, mouths blowing smoke up one another's nostrils as they chatted. A thick, greasy smell greeted me as the doorbell clanged and I went in. Several folk looked up then down again like robots programmed to spot a newcomer.

'Tea, please.' I gave the woman behind the counter a pound coin.

'Just got off the train?' She poured a mug of tea so strong you could dye your hair with it and shoved a fifty pence piece back at me.

I told her I had. Then I decided to show her James's

picture. After all that's what I had come for so I might as well start right away.

I fished it out of my bag. 'I'm looking for a friend,' I told her, showing it to her. 'This is him. I don't suppose you've seen him, have you?'

She peered at it then shook her head. 'Most of the youngsters hang around the arcade. You could look there.'

'Thanks.' I put it back in my pocket. I felt disappointed even though I knew it was stupid to dream the first person I asked would have seen him.

The only seat vacant was one next to a smelly old man who sat mumbling to himself. He had a couple of shopping bags beside him, crammed full of what looked like old socks. I pulled the chair to one side so I wouldn't have to sit too close to him. He glanced at me, scanning, bleary eyes under a mop of grey hair. I looked away, embarrassed and scared.

Suddenly someone called out, 'Whoa, Jimmy, looks like your luck's in.' The voice came from a table in the corner by the window. There were two guys sitting there, scruffy looking and dressed in tatty old jeans and combat jackets. A black dog lay asleep half under the table, its tail twitching as it chased rabbits in its sleep. There was another boy with them but he had his head on the table, fast asleep. Or so I thought at the time. Although later, when I'd had a chance to think about it and I'd got to know a different Dartcombe from the one James had fantasized about, I decided he'd probably been stoned.

Jimmy stopped mumbling when he heard the shout. Then suddenly he jumped up out of his chair so violently it fell back with a clang, hitting one of the women sitting behind him. 'Hey, watch it, you silly old sod.' She gave Jimmy a shove and he stumbled away. I cringed, looking the other way as if I hadn't even noticed what was happening. I felt sorry for the old man—he was obviously out of it.

'Don't run away from her, Jimmy,' one of the young guys shouted as Jimmy headed for the door clutching his sock bags as if they were life support systems. 'It could be your lucky night.'

I decided not to hang around. I gulped down my tea, picked up my rucksack and hurried out. One of the young guys put his arm out to stop me. He looked at me with bright eyes under a curtain of dull dreadlocks. 'What's the hurry?'

I shrugged, still scared. I must have been nuts to come into a place like this. 'Nothing.'

'Stay and have another drink.'

I edged away from his hand. 'No thanks.' I wrenched open the door and shot outside colliding with a passer-by and almost knocking her over.

She grabbed my arm to steady me. 'Hey, what's the rush?'

'Thanks,' I said when I got my balance back. I felt a real idiot. 'Sorry.'

I looked up to see a girl of about twenty grinning at me. Her face was dead pale under spiky orange hair. She had a ring through one eyebrow and one nostril and had on a black leather jacket, black leggings, and rainbow Doc Martens.

'Giving you hassle in there, were they?' she asked, still grinning.

I managed a grin back. 'Kind of.' I went to pick up my bag where it had flown from my hand and gone spinning into the gutter. I brushed off the mud and rainwater.

'Visitor are you?' she asked.

I nodded. 'Yeah.'

'What brings you to a dump like this?' she asked.

I told her and showed her James's photo. She shook her head, pulling a face. 'Can't say I've seen anyone who particularly looks like him,' she said. 'Take a look down the Front.'

'I'm going to,' I said.

She walked along with me. 'My name's Roz,' she said. 'What's yours?'

I told her.

'What you looking for this boy for?'

So I told her that too. It seemed crazy talking like that to a complete stranger but she seemed really interested and she just might be the person I needed to help me.

She chuckled when I told her about James coming here as a kid and what a great place it had been to come for your holidays.

'It doesn't exactly look like that now,' I commented.

Roz shrugged. 'It's not really a bad place to hang out,' she said. 'You don't get hassled too much, yeah, it's good. Just not the kind of place it used to be when your friend was a kid, that's all. Things change.'

'Yeah,' I said. 'Obviously.'

As we got near the Front I could see what she meant. Half the shops were closed and shuttered and those that were open looked poor and neglected. I had a sudden vision of the town where I lived. Nice shops, nice streets, nice park. Nice houses except the grotty estate where James lived. This was like being on another planet.

We walked past a row of offices, closed up and empty. Falling to bits by the look of the rubble lying around the pavement in front. And as we went through a side street and came out into the road that ran along the beach I could see the pier. The end was a blackened mass of twisted girders.

Roz must have seen me looking shocked. 'Caught fire last year,' she told me. 'I don't suppose they'll ever do it up.'

Misery washed over me. Poor James. If he *was* here then his dreams would have turned to dust. I began to cry. Silently in the hope Roz wouldn't notice. But she did.

She put her arm round me. 'Hey, don't cry.'

'Sorry.' I felt a fool, crying in front of a complete

stranger. I sniffed and dragged a tissue from my pocket. 'I just feel sorry for James, that's all.'

'Look,' Roz said, 'why don't you come back to my place? You can start looking for your mate later when the weather clears up.'

I shook my head again. 'No, thanks all the same. I want to try to find him as soon as I can.'

She shrugged. 'OK. But look, if you need a place to stay . . . '

'I thought I'd find a B and B somewhere,' I told her.

She gazed at me. 'You got money, then?'

'Fifty quid,' I said.

'Oh.' Her eyebrows shot up. 'Well, you'll be lucky if you find anywhere open but you can try, I suppose.'

'Oh.' Stupidly, I'd thought finding somewhere to stay would be easy. I should have realized most places would be closed this time of the year.

She was still staring at me. 'But if you can't, come to my place. I'm in a squat along the Front just the other side of the pier.'

'A squat?' I said. 'Oh . . . right . . . thanks.'

'It's got posters stuck all over the boards,' she explained. 'You know, rock gigs and all that. Come round the back. I've got a whole room to myself and my mattress is big enough for both of us.' She grinned.

I grinned back. 'Thanks.'

I watched her stride off along the pavement. I felt better. Dartcombe might be a grotty place but I felt I'd found a friend already.

I mooched along the seafront, trying to decide what to do next. A little way out, a whole bunch of screaming gulls were whirling and diving over the snow-capped breakers. Then I spotted a couple of people across the road. They were huddled in a bus shelter. I decided to ask them if they'd seen James.

The wind was so strong it seemed to be trying to stop me crossing the road. I turned my collar up against it and fought my way across to the other side.

The shelter was littered with lager cans and rubbish. It smelt terrible, as if someone had used it as a lavatory. The people in there were two women, both looking pinched and cold.

I went and sat beside them. 'Do you live in Dartcombe?' I asked.

They both stared at me, suspiciously, then glanced at each other. One wore a clear polythene rain hat over blue-rinsed hair. The other had on a kind of white fake-fur hat that looked like a drowned cat.

'We can't give you any money,' Drowned Cat said quickly.

'Money?' I wasn't really sure what she was on about.

'Yes. We haven't got any.' They suddenly seemed to be huddling together scared of something. I realized it was me.

I shook my head. 'It's OK, thanks. I've already got some.'

'What do you want then?' Polythene Bag asked warily. She was obviously convinced I was out to mug them. Then, braver, she went on. 'You people are always begging. You should get jobs then you'd have enough to live on,' she added quickly as if it had taken a great effort to say it and she had to get it out fast before she lost courage.

I shook my head. They'd got totally the wrong end of the stick. 'No . . . ' I fished James's photo out of my pocket. 'I just wanted to ask you if you'd seen this boy, that's all. He's run away from home and I'm trying to find him.' The picture was a bit screwed up from being taken in and out of my pocket but they stared at it for a minute just the same.

They seemed to relax a bit. Polythene Bag pushed the dripping edge of her hat back from the top rim of her glasses to get a better look.

Then they both shook their heads. 'No,' they said both at the same time. 'Never set eyes on him.'

'Are you sure?'

'Quite sure,' Drowned Cat said.

I sighed. 'OK, thanks.'

Then the lights of a bus trundled out of the gloom and stopped with a hiss of brakes. The two women couldn't get on it quick enough. I saw one staring at me as it pulled away. Staring at me as if I was an alien.

I left the bus shelter and headed for the arcade. At least in there it would be warm and dry.

On the way, I passed a burger place and suddenly realized I was starving. I'd been too up tight to get anything on the train, even though a man had come round with a trolley of sandwiches and snacks. So the last thing I'd had was breakfast at home. It seemed a million miles away.

It was almost dark and the street lights sparkled above wet pavements. I wondered if I should phone home. Mum and Dad would have found my note by now and would be going spare. I'd been so moody and miserable they might be thinking I'd run away for good. And maybe I had. Although I didn't think Dartcombe was the place to find your dreams.

I went into the burger place and used the loo then got a takeaway. There was a crowd of teenagers sitting at a table by the window. They were having a great time, laughing and joking, one of them messing around with a napkin, making a paper dart. One had his back to me . . . dark hair curling over his collar and for one, soaring moment I thought it might be James. But when he turned sideways I saw he had a long pointed nose and sun-tanned skin. I turned, disappointed. One of them threw me a glance as I went out but the others didn't even look.

The arcade was packed. I guessed the owner prayed for days like this when people wanted to be indoors. I finished my burger and stuffed the package into the overflowing litter bin. Then I wandered around, stopping now and then to show people James's picture. Some just shrugged and shook their heads, others took time to study it. But no one had seen him. Not one single person.

I hung around beside the Grand Prix machine by the door, glancing at everyone as they came in. It was dark now, the cold wind still blowing the litter around. A pile of it lay in a soggy mess against the corner of the doorway. A little way along, the jagged outline of the pier was stark against the sky.

I wondered what James would do if he did come in and find me there. He'd never believe it was really me. I tried to imagine where he would be and what he would be doing. I was feeling really fed up. It was three days since he had left home, surely if he was here, *someone* would have spotted him by now?

'Any luck?' I recognized Roz's voice behind me. I turned, managing a small grin and a shrug. A vague thought that she had followed me there flitted through my mind.

'Nope. I've asked loads of people. No one's seen him.'

'Did you find somewhere to stay?' She didn't take her eyes off my face.

I shrugged again. By now I hardly cared where I slept. 'No.'

'What you going to do?'

I shrugged again. 'No idea.'

'Poor Cass.' She put her arm across my shoulders. 'You look shattered. Why don't you come home with me? You can start asking round again in the morning.'

I sighed. 'Yeah, OK.' Then I remembered my parents. They'd really be going frantic by now. 'Have you got a phone I could use?' I asked her.

'A phone?' she laughed. 'You've got to be joking. But there's a box not far away.'

'OK.'

We walked along the Front then up a side road, through a series of narrow lanes with shops either side then into a square. An alleyway off it led back down to the seafront.

The phone box was right in the middle of it.

'Won't be a minute,' I said. For some reason or other my heart was beating like a wild drum. I knew what Mum would say. I knew she'd be out of her mind with worry. I knew she'd try to make me tell them where I was . . . to hang on . . . they'd come and get me. But I couldn't go back. Not until I'd found James. I had to try and do something right. I would explain and make them understand.

But I didn't get the chance. The box had been vandalized, the receiver on the floor, smashed to bits. When I came out again, Roz just shrugged as if she had known all along that it would be.

Bordering the square was a huge old-fashioned building, rows of wide bay windows all boarded up. It looked as if it might have been nice—about a hundred years ago.

Roz threw her arms out wide. 'Home,' she said. 'Great, huh?'

Right then I was too tired and too weary to care. I couldn't help worrying about Mum and Dad though. I was trying desperately not to but I couldn't help it. I *should* have phoned earlier. It seemed I was just proving that I was really nothing but a dead loss. I couldn't even get *this* right.

We went round the back. Roz pushed aside a board nailed to the back entrance and squeezed through. I clambered in behind her. We were in a huge entrance hall, gloomy and cobweb ridden in the light that came through from a window above the staircase. But even in the murkiness I could see it had once been rich and elegant. There were plaster mouldings on the ceiling and a round, stained-glass window above the door.

'Wow!' I looked around. 'What *was* this place?'

'The Grand Hotel,' Roz grinned. 'Not grand now, is it?'

'Hardly.'

'It's due for demolition,' she said, 'but the stupid

council can't agree on plans for redevelopment. Still,' she added, 'does us a favour.'

'Us?'

'Yeah, there's loads of us here, didn't I say?'

I shook my head. Then, as if to prove she was telling the truth a bloke came clattering down the bare wooden stairs. He had long hair tied back in a ponytail and wore tight jeans under a tatty army T-shirt. He had friendship bands halfway up to his elbow.

'Jed,' Roz said. 'This is Cass, she's come to stay with me.'

'Great.' Jed gave me a nod as he looked me up and down. 'Parents chuck you out?'

I shook my head. 'No.'

'Trouble with the law? School?'

I shook my head again, suddenly shy because of the way he was staring at me.

Roz fumbled in the inside of her jacket, took out something and handed it to Jed. 'See you later?' she said.

She led me up the rickety stairs, along several corridors and into her room.

'The loo's at the end.' She pointed into the gloom. 'It doesn't flush so we have to get a bucket of water from the public one down the road and tip that down it. It's best not to use it unless you have to.'

'Right,' I said in a small voice.

Inside, she lit several candles. There was a mattress on the floor, a box with a clock and a copy of the *Big Issue* on it, a pile of clothes on the floor . . . nothing else. It was cold and damp and ratty. And it smelt. Although it faced the sea, the window was covered by boards so you couldn't see out. I shivered as Roz plonked herself down on the mattress and covered herself with a blanket, pulling it up over her shoulders and round under her chin. I could see she had started to shiver too. She must have seen me looking horrified. 'Not exactly the Ritz, is it?' Her teeth were chattering as she spoke.

I managed a kind of stupefied grin. 'No.'

'It's better than some have got,' she said.

'Is it?' I said thinking nothing in the world could be much worse.

'Yeah. Old Jimmy, that crazy bloke who came out of the café just before you. He lives under the pier.'

'Oh, God,' I said. 'How awful.' I had a vision of him huddled up on the pebbles, the wind whipping pain into his old bones. 'Why can't he come here?' I shivered again. If James was in Dartcombe he might be having to sleep on the beach. Or in some cold doorway somewhere. It wasn't likely he'd got any money. My heart did a great lurch. He could get attacked, picked up by the police . . . anything if he was sleeping rough.

Roz shrugged. 'He's out of it half the time. He used to live in a home but they threw him out. Care in the community and all that stuff.'

'Who looks after him, then?'

'That's it,' she said. 'No one. There's a couple of hostels but you have to be there early to get in. He's supposed to take medication but he prefers booze.'

'Hostels?' I said. 'Where are they?'

'Round the back streets,' Roz told me. 'One used to be a church, they've converted it.'

I turned. There hadn't been much point in standing in front of the window anyway. All you could make out was a glimmer of light peeking through the boards. This place would give me claustrophobia if I stayed here long. I felt suddenly as if I really was on another planet, my warm cosy house and family a million light years away.

Roz patted the mattress. 'Come on, you'll freeze. You'll have to use your jacket as a pillow, I've only got one.'

I crept in beside her. I hadn't washed or cleaned my teeth or anything. I felt a wreck, dirty, shivery . . . hungry in spite of my takeaway. I wanted to go to the loo too but felt I'd rather die than use one that wouldn't flush. As night slithered in, the hum of the traffic gradually died. I could hear the sound of the surf pounding the beach like a distant rumour of guns. I remembered what James had said about waking up and hearing the sea. Somehow I didn't think this is what he had in mind.

Roz had slumped back against her pillow, staring up at the candle-shadowed ceiling. I could feel the side of her body against mine. Although she was trembling there was a kind of heat coming off her. I could smell she had been sweating as if she had a fever. I hoped she wasn't sick. Not only for her sake but for mine too. The last thing I wanted was to pick up some virus or other when I was so far away from home.

Roz shifted so she was closer still. It felt good to have someone beside me. When I was small I used to creep into Mum and Dad's bed some mornings. I remembered lying there, giant sleepy bodies against mine. It had seemed like the heaven that James dreamed of. I felt a great gap of loneliness opening up inside me. If I didn't watch out I'd fall in and drown. Then, suddenly and without any warning at all I began to cry again. I felt stupid but I couldn't help it. Roz would think I did nothing but weep.

'Hey, Cass.' She put her arm round me.

I wiped my face on my sleeve. 'Sorry,' I said. 'I've been having a bit of a rough time lately, that's all. I'm just being a wimp, ignore me.'

Her hand stroked my hair and tucked a lock of it behind my ear. 'I thought it was your mate who was having a rough time.'

'Yeah. Him as well,' I said.

'How old are you?' she asked.

I told her.

'You're just a kid,' she said.

'Am I?' I knew I sounded bitter. What she said was true, though. I *was* a kid but sometimes I felt as old as time.

Roz propped herself up on one elbow. 'Get some sleep, Cass,' she said softly. 'You'll feel better in the morning.' I felt her shiver as she sat up and clasped her arms round her bent knees. I wanted to ask her if she was sick but I was just going to when she got up suddenly and began walking around the room. Up and down, up and down. I could hear her humming to herself, a tuneless tune that went on and on. Then I must have dozed off.

A bit later, when I awoke, I heard people talking in low voices on the other side of the room.

Roz. 'You were gone a long time.'

The other was Jed. 'Sorry . . . not my fault.'

I opened my eyes. They were sitting on the floor, cross-legged. I could smell something burning. A horrible, bitter smell that made me want to heave. They had a lighted candle in front of them and Jed was holding something over it. A shiny piece of paper with white powder in it. I heard Roz say, 'Hurry up, Jed, for Christ's sake.'

I went cold. As if a winter wind had suddenly come through the shutters and turned the room to ice. They were using drugs. I'd seen stuff about it on TV and read about it at school too. I began shivering uncontrollably. Roz must have seen because after a minute or two she got up and came over to me. 'Cass, you awake?'

But I was too scared to answer her. Instead I turned over and mumbled something. I hoped she'd think I was having a bad dream. There certainly weren't any dreamcatchers here to filter them out. She pulled the blanket up over my shoulders and went back to Jed. I could hear them talking, a low laugh and a rustle now and then. Then they both got up and went out. I could hear them clattering down the stairs talking loudly, excitedly, leaving me totally alone with my stupidity.

10

It wasn't until I was streets away from that place that I found my fifty quid had gone. I felt so stupid I could have died.

There'd been no sign of anyone when I woke up, cold and stiff as a frozen chicken from my night on the floor. I was glad. Roz had been kind to me but I didn't ever want to see her again. All I wanted to do was find James.

I was looking in my rucksack for my purse when I realized it had gone. I was walking along the seafront at the time. At least the rain had cleared and it was a bright, light morning. The tide was out, the dazzling sea a mirror in the sun. There were lots of people down on the beach. Walking dogs, some just walking. Near the sea's edge a couple of dark figures were digging for worms. Dartcombe didn't look quite so bad in the early morning light.

When I couldn't locate my purse I put my bag down on a seat and dragged everything out desperately. T-shirt, pants, wash-stuff, strewn all over the place. I took out my dreamcatcher and realized another nightmare had somehow got through. My purse wasn't there. Roz must have taken it while I was asleep. It could only have been her . . . or Jed, I hadn't let my bag out of my sight until then.

I suddenly felt so angry I could have yelled and screamed. I'd thought she was my friend. How stupid could you get.

I stuffed everything back in. At least I had James's photo in my pocket. At least that was safe. I had a few odd bits of change too. Enough to buy me something to eat and phone home. It seemed like a defeat though. Just for once I'd wanted to do something right and I'd even mucked that up.

I found a public loo and managed to wash my face and hands, shivering under the freezing water that gushed from the tap. I went into one of the cubicles to wash the other parts of me. Then I changed into my jeans and dragged a brush through my hair. In the mirror I looked ghastly. As if I'd just been dug up. My hair was stringy and needed washing. I had dark shadows under my eyes and a spot on my chin. In total—a wreck.

In a seafront café I asked the man behind the counter and showed him James's picture. He hadn't seen him, but suggested I went to the hostel.

'Most homeless youngsters get a night or two's stay,' he told me as he poured me a cup of tea. He must have come from Greece or somewhere because he had an accent as thick as treacle.

I counted out my change. Just enough for tea and a round of toast. He stared at the pathetic coins on the palm of my hand. 'Is that all you got?'

I nodded. 'Just about.'

He must have taken pity on me because he cooked me an egg to go with my toast.

On the way to the hostel I thought I spotted Roz. In the distance. Someone just like her was talking to a man washing his car in the road outside a block of flats. My heart began its wild beat as I dashed towards her. I knew I should have gone to the police and reported her pinching my fifty quid but I was too scared they'd try to make me go home. But I wasn't too scared to ask her for it back.

But it wasn't her at all. Up close, it wasn't even like her. I must have been wishing so hard I'd hallucinated. Even if it had been she would have denied it. I knew I'd never get the money back anyway. She would have already used it to get drugs. I seethed with helpless anger when I thought about it. The couple stared at me curiously but I just walked on by. They obviously thought I was some batty teenager, racing up to them then stopping dead and walking away.

I tried to concentrate my mind on finding James and nothing else. Because that was the only thing that really mattered. Fifty quid . . . a night on a druggie's floor. It would have been worth it if only I could find him.

The hostel still looked like a church outside. In fact I thought I was in the wrong place until I saw a board that said 'Men's Hostel' propped up against the wall. Grey flints, gothic windows. Steps up to a huge wooden front door with a great black knocker and a letter box. I always thought it was weird, churches having letter boxes. After all, no one lived in them. Only God and it wasn't any use writing to Him.

I stood there looking, imagining brides walking up the steps, white trains flowing. Funeral processions with flowers and people in black. All there would be now would be a procession of homeless, hopeless people seeking shelter for the night. I decided that's what all churches should be for. It was OK believing in God but it didn't keep you warm on a bitter winter's night or fill your stomach with hot soup if you were starving hungry.

The door was locked but there was a button to press to speak to someone inside. I pressed it and said what I wanted. After about five minutes, someone came out. A thin young man with piercing blue eyes and pale hair down to his shoulders.

'Sorry,' he said. 'Phone rang just as I was coming out. I'm Doug, what can I do for you?'

I showed him James's picture. 'I wondered if he's been here?'

He took it from me and peered at it for a second or two. Then he shook his head. 'No, sorry. At least, not while I've been on duty.'

My heart sank to the soles of my boots. 'Oh,' I said dismally. 'Well, thanks anyway.'

He must have seen the look on my face. 'Hey, don't give up just yet.' He stood back so I could go inside. 'We keep a record of everyone who stays here. If he did come then his name might be in it.'

I followed him into what used to be the vestry. There was a desk covered with a million bits of paper and a notice board with posters on. Posters with pictures of people gazing out at me. I stared back. *Missing*, most of them said. Others . . . *Have you seen this boy . . . girl . . . man . . . woman . . . ?* Photos of ordinary looking people like me and James. Seeing them made me feel sadder than I'd ever been in my life.

Doug must have seen me staring. 'Not one of James there is there?'

I shook my head. 'No. He hasn't been gone long. No one's put posters out or anything. I just came by myself, hoping to find him.'

'Bit like looking for a needle in a haystack,' Doug commented.

I sighed. 'Yeah. I'm beginning to find that out. But I'm really worried about James. I'm scared he'll get tangled up with druggies or someone who'll hurt him. He pretends to be tough but he isn't really.'

Doug was looking through a book with lots of handwriting in it. He looked up.

'Yeah,' he said. 'Don't we all.' Then he shook his head. 'No luck, I'm afraid. There's no James Derwent in here. Mind you, lots won't give their names. Especially if they don't want to be traced. And we don't ask. We're here to give shelter not to ask questions.'

I heaved a sigh. 'No, I suppose not.'

'What makes you think he might be in Dartcombe?' Doug asked.

I told him. 'He loved it here,' I said. 'It was his dream.'

Doug chuckled. 'And now it's his nightmare?'

I shrugged. 'I don't know. If I could find him then I'd ask him.'

Doug closed the book. He shook his head. 'People come down here thinking there's lots of casual jobs they can do, but it's not that easy.'

'No,' I said.

'All the temporary work finishes at the end of the season and then there's nothing.' He shook his head again and sighed. 'Then they end up on the streets. We help as many as we can but sometimes I reckon we're fighting a losing battle.'

'Yes,' I said stupidly. Hearing about this was like hearing about life on another planet. I *knew* lots of people were homeless but had never really thought about how they got that way.

I reckoned I must have been living in some kind of bubble. Maybe that's what my dreamcatcher had done. Instead of filtering out dreams it had filtered out reality. The only thing that had escaped the net was getting pregnant.

'So they get into a vicious circle,' Doug went on. 'Alcohol and drugs to try to cheer themselves up. Then they can't feel good without them. They just end up in a spiral into misery.'

'Oh, God . . . poor James.' I shook my head. 'I just don't know what to do now.'

'You'll just have to keep asking around, that's all,' Doug advised. 'This isn't a huge place. People come here because rooms are cheap and the police are pretty tolerant. You might be lucky.'

'If he does come, will you tell him I'm here in town looking for him,' I said.

'Sure I will, no problem. Have you tried the police at all?'

I shook my head. 'No, but I might do now.'

'It might be an idea. Have you got anywhere to stay tonight?' Doug wanted to know.

I shook my head then told him about Roz.

He shook *his* head and pulled a face. Then he told me about the women's hostel. 'But you'd be better phoning your parents to come and get you.'

'No,' I said. 'Not yet.'

I felt worse than ever when I left the hostel. Doug had showed me round. It was better than the streets but it still filled me with horror. Beds packed like sardines, grey blankets, the smell. Doug gave me the address of the women's hostel and told me to go there.

'Don't stay out all night,' he warned. 'It's pretty dangerous.'

When I left, my heart was a great lump of lead weighing me down. I *had* to find James. I had to get it right.

Walking back along the street I suddenly realized something. It had been at least another twenty-four hours since I'd thought about Steve and the *operation* and how miserable I was about everything. I realized something else too. My mum had been right. It wasn't the end of the world. I'd got to get on with my life.

But first . . . I had to find James.

I spent the whole day scouring the town. I went in every shop, every café, every bank, every building society, hairdresser, every pub. I didn't care any longer whether people thought I was a pain or not. But no one had seen James. No one at all. I still couldn't pluck up the courage to go into the police station. I didn't really know why. It just seemed as if I would be making James into a criminal if I went there even though he had done nothing wrong.

By six o'clock I was shattered. I stumbled back down to the seafront. I was starving hungry, cold, tired and fed up. I had nowhere to spend the night and didn't really care if I slept under the pier like old Jimmy from the café. Only when I really thought about it I shivered with more than cold. I couldn't even be bothered to find the women's hostel Doug had told me about.

I decided to go along to the arcade again. It was

already dark although the street lights of the town threw an orange glow into the sky. I walked along the sea wall. The sparkle from the promenade lamps caught now and then the foam of the crested waves and flicked them on and off.

The arcade manager must have thought I was up to something when I crossed the road and began hanging around the doorway and not playing the machines. When he came up to me I showed him James's picture. He hadn't been around when I'd gone there before.

Needless to say he hadn't seen him. 'You look cold,' he said when he'd given it back to me. He looked me up and down.

I huddled into my collar. 'I'm freezing.' I knew I looked more of a wreck than ever. Red nose, white face, hair stringier than it had been that morning. A walking nightmare. I felt ill too. Hungry, sick, and scared.

'Come in the back,' the guy said, taking pity on me. He jangled his long chain of machine keys in his hand up and down, up and down as if he was composing a tune. 'I'll make you a cup of tea.'

I hadn't had anything to drink for hours and I couldn't say no even though I'd got a horrible, sneaky feeling I'd regret it But the place was packed so I imagined I'd be OK.

'All right,' I said stupidly. 'Thanks.'

Passing the change kiosk, he said something to the bloke inside but there was so much noise from the machines that I couldn't hear what it was. Only 'OK, Frank,' and a wink at me as I went by.

There was a cosy little room with a kettle and mugs and an electric fire. It smelt of stale nicotine but I was so grateful for the warmth I wouldn't have cared *what* it stank of. I sat down on a sagging pink sofa that had definitely seen better days.

'Fag?' Frank dragged a crumpled packet from his jeans pocket and waved it at me.

'No, thanks.'

He put a mug of tea in front of me. 'Sugar?'

'No, thanks.'

'So you're looking for your boyfriend?'

'That's right.' The mug was warming my numb fingers, warming my frozen heart. I was too weary to explain that James wasn't my *boyfriend*, just my *friend*.

'Ditched you, has he?' Frank grinned.

'Ditched me?' Then I smiled back. 'No, he's . . . ' Then I told him James had run away from home.

Frank sat back in the corner of the sofa, one leg crossed over the other, blowing smoke through his mouth and nostrils. He pulled off his jacket. Underneath he'd got on a sleeveless vest and had tattoos on his arms. A dragon, a lion, Elvis on the back of his hand. I noticed he wasn't wearing socks and his legs above the cuff of his trainers were covered in black hairs.

'This place is full of kids like that. Don't know what attracts them.'

I shrugged. I didn't know either.

'What you going to do if you don't find him?' Frank asked.

I shrugged again. 'I don't know.'

'Go back home to Mummy and Daddy?'

I flinched at the tone of his voice. I didn't know why he was speaking like that. Maybe he'd summed me up as a poor little rich girl. How wrong could anyone be.

I shrugged again. 'I suppose so.'

Frank put down his mug and leaned forward. 'Have you got anywhere to stay tonight?'

'No, not yet.'

'Stay here if you want. It's warm and cosy. I often kip down here.'

I was suddenly, stupidly, belatedly, scared. 'Er . . . that's kind, but . . . ' I began in my silly, polite, small-town voice. I realized I wanted to be out of there. The prospect of a night on the cold and desolate beach suddenly seemed the most inviting thing in the world.

Frank flung out his hand and touched my arm. 'Hey, come on.'

I looked down at the picture of Elvis. His face seemed to be moving, smiling, as Frank's fingers slithered over the satin of my sleeve.

I gulped the last of my tea. 'No, thanks . . . honestly . . . ' I started to get up but he had already sidled so close he could grab me with both hands.

'Come on,' he said and I could tell he was getting hot and irritated. 'You're a nice kid . . . you don't want to be out on your own all night, surely?'

'It's OK.' I tried to wriggle out of his grasp. 'I'll go to the hostel . . . '

He grunted. 'Hostel? Stinking women in stinking beds when you could be here with me.' He grinned again then reached up to stroke my hair, his eyes running over my face. 'You're not that daft, are you?'

My heart was thudding so boisterously it hurt. I wrenched away from him and scrambled up. But that was totally the wrong thing to do. He was up with me, pulling me to him and pressing the whole of his foul body against mine. I must have been totally, utterly mad to come out the back with him. I could see that now. It had got to be a habit, realizing how stupid I was when it was already too late.

I felt his face in my hair, his hands searching under my jacket, pulling, kneading, pressing . . . Then he grabbed a fistful of my hair and pulled my head back. 'If you need a bed for the night you really should earn it,' he said, his voice thick and oily. 'You don't get something for nothing in this world. Didn't Mummy ever tell you that?'

'I'm not that desperate.' I put my hands against his chest and pushed as hard as I could. 'You're a bloody pervert,' I said although I knew he wasn't a pervert at all. I'd been stupid enough to go out the back with him when I should have realized what he wanted me to do.

I was still trying to shove him away. 'I'll yell and scream,' I threatened.

He laughed. 'Who do you think's going to hear you above that racket?'

I knew he was right. I could scream my head off and no one would hear. He was so close I could smell the sweat under his arms, the tobacco on his breath. For one horrible minute I thought I was going to throw up. I glared at him, trying to kid him it was anger he could see in my eyes, not fear.

Suddenly, he let me go. So abruptly I almost fell over. I put my hand out to stop myself falling backwards on to the settee.

I pulled my jacket down, grabbed my bag and headed for the door, reaching desperately for the handle that would lead me to safety.

Frank had sat down and lit another cigarette. 'Push off,' he said sulkily, not looking at me but staring into the depths of the electric fire. 'And I don't want to see you hanging around here again.'

'No chance!' I wrenched open the door and slammed out. I stood outside for a minute trying to get my breath. My heart was still pounding and my knees felt like jelly. I felt a fool. Everyone would know what had happened. But no one was taking any notice at all. They were all too intent on the machines. The man in the change kiosk had his nose stuck in the *Daily Star* and didn't look up once.

I staggered out, pushing through, almost knocking people down. One or two shouted at me as I banged into them. As I ran like the wind across the road and down to the beach their voices echoed in my ears. I hared down the steps, two at a time, almost tripping again through the blur of my stupid tears.

I stumbled down to the water's edge. Then plonked down on the pebbles. The waves were breaking so close I could feel the salt spray on my face. I hugged my knees and stared out to sea. Gradually my heart calmed

108

and my shaking stopped. There was a ship on the horizon, winking its lights at me. Close by was the scarred pier, a sad reminder of Dartcombe in its heyday. It was hard to imagine it ever had one.

I put my hands in my pockets and hunched myself up against the cold wind that was blowing terror and hate into my heart. My fingers closed over a ten pence piece. My very last coin. I could go now . . . use it to phone Mum and Dad . . . beg them to come and get me, take me away from this ghastly place. I could at last admit defeat.

I put my forehead into my knees. It was the only thing I could do. James wasn't here. I'd been wasting my time.

When I looked up, the great grey eye of the moon was looking at me through scudding clouds. I could make out the man in the moon's nose, his mouth. When I was little I always believed it really was a man's face. When people argued I told them you could see it, every detail etched in silver. Just as I had believed the dreamcatcher sifted out the bad ones. Now I knew that both things were a lie.

There was a noise behind me and a crowd of people came galloping down the beach, laughing and chucking cans at one another. They didn't notice me there, huddled by the ocean's edge. Either it was too dark or I was too small, I didn't know. But wasn't that what I had wanted all along? To shrink and disappear from everyone's sight for ever?

11

I don't know how long I sat there before I realized that I was so cold it felt my bones were freezing. I hunched up, hugging myself, but it didn't make any difference. The sky was a deep velvet blue, the sparkling stars a blizzard.

By the pier, a ragged group of people had built a fire. I could see its sharp flames, a slug-trail of silver smoke creeping into the night sky. They huddled around it clutching cans of lager and bottles of something or other as if they were their life support systems. They looked like Native Americans having a powwow. I'd read in one of my books that in certain peoples, their medicine men can see the future in the embers of a fire. It seemed to me that these people didn't have a future at all, and maybe no past either. All they had was now.

Their voices drifted towards me on the night air, the echoes splashing into the waves and getting washed away. I wanted to go and ask them if I could warm myself but I was scared. Then, gradually, I realized that if I didn't, I would probably die of exposure. So I got up and stumbled over, not caring whether they were dangerous or not.

They hardly even looked up when I reached them. They didn't ask me anything. Who was I? Where did I come from? What I was doing there? They weren't even curious about me. One or two just shifted closer together so there was room for me to squat. There were three men and two women. Bundled up in scarves and thick old army coats, gloves with no fingers. Their piled-up belongings a rag-bag mountain on the pebbles. I sat down, hugging my bag. One handed me a bottle. First I shook my head but then as he thrust it closer I took it and gulped a swig. Whisky. It burned my throat and warmed the cold caverns of my heart.

'Thanks.' I handed the bottle back.

One of the men was telling a story. It was about his dog, how he had left it behind when his wife threw him out. Leaving it broke his heart, he said. He couldn't have looked after it, he had nowhere to go.

'Poor old Robbie,' one of the women said. 'Pining for a dog when it's supposed to be the other way round.'

Everyone laughed, their hoots and cackles echoing across the water. Everyone that was, except me. I knew what it was like to be desperately sad about something you hadn't been able to keep.

It went quiet then. There was only the sound of the sea. There's a certain hush about a calm sea at night. A shallow shooshing and sheeshing. Maybe people have sat near the ocean for millions of years, letting the soft sound calm their minds. I and the others round the fire were just minute grains of sand on a beach as wide as the universe.

Someone else began telling a story of his life. He had a broad Scottish accent and I could hardly understand what he was saying. What I did understand though, was that these were just ordinary people, like me and James, who'd got swept away on the tide of their own lives and couldn't find their way back. I didn't even know why I'd been scared of them.

I must have gone to sleep after that. The last thing I remembered was more loud laughter and jeering, the sound of a distant motorbike fracturing the air. I was leaning my cheek against the rough material of the shoulder next to me. Then it drifted away as I dozed.

When I woke up, my companions were stretched at various angles on the beach, fanned out like the spokes of a wheel. The fire was out. I was stiff and sore and so starving hungry the noises in my stomach were louder than their snores.

I got to my feet and left them there to sleep away the day.

As the sun rose, the frost on the railings turned to pale, rising ghosts. A hop of sparrows was rummaging round beneath the hot dog stall. They rose as I passed with sudden bright wingbeats into the morning sky. I crossed the road and went into the café. The owner was there, heating the grills for early breakfasts. He let me use the loo.

When I came out, I told him I was going home.

'Given up looking for your friend, then?' He was unloading eggs from the fridge.

'I haven't really given up,' I told him. 'I just don't know what else to do.'

'You could go to the police,' he suggested.

I shook my head. 'I don't think there's really any point.'

'Oh, well. Maybe you get home and he be there already,' the man said. I could tell he was trying to cheer me up.

'I don't know,' I said sadly. 'I hope so.' Somehow, though, I doubted it.

My fingers closed over the ten pence piece in my pocket. It was my ticket home.

The nearest unvandalized phone box was at the railway station. I tramped there. I felt so unhappy I hadn't found James, I could have wept. I had wanted to more than anything else in the world.

The phone box was being used so I hung around outside. Although the sun was up it was still cold. I hugged myself, stamping my feet to try to get warm.

The person using the box came out at last. Inside it smelt of urine and fag ash. The phone was still warm. I dialled, imagining Mum or Dad rushing downstairs to answer it. When I heard Dad's voice I stuck in the coin. My heart was thumping so loudly the glass walls of the box were almost vibrating with the thunder of its beats.

'Dad,' I said. 'It's me.'

'Cass!' I could hear fear and relief in his voice. 'Cass, where are you?'

I told him.

'Dartcombe? Oh, Cass, are you OK? We've been going frantic.'

'I know, Dad. Look, I've only got 10p. Can you come and get me?'

Then I heard Mum, breathless, scared. 'Is it Cass? Where is she? Is she all right?' I could imagine her, hair all over the place, old T-shirt she wore as a nightie. Suddenly, I wanted to cry.

'Yes, she's fine,' I heard Dad say even though I hadn't said whether I was or not. 'Cass, whereabouts are you?'

'I'm at the railway station ' Then there were some clicks and pips and the line went dead. I put the receiver down with a sigh. Ten pence between life and death. I'd just have to hang around until they turned up.

I sat on one of the seats outside. I knew I'd got a long wait. It would take hours to get there by road. Rush hour, traffic accidents, road works. I'd just have to be patient. I imagined Dad driving like a maniac, Mum not telling him to slow down for a change. I could see her face, white and anxious, frightened that when they arrived they wouldn't be able to find me. Asking Dad if he was sure he knew the way. Him telling her to shut up—of course he did.

The station was getting busy, people coming and going, being dropped off for trains, coming to Dartcombe to work. I sat huddled into my collar.

A policeman came up to me.

'Are you waiting for someone?' he asked. 'You've been here an hour.'

He must have been spying on me.

'Yeah,' I said. 'My parents.'

'And you're all right, are you?' He eyed my scruffy

hair and dirty, creased clothes. I looked a homeless wreck, just emerged from some doorway or other to spend the day on the station seat. For some strange reason I suddenly wanted him to know my reason for being here.

I fished James's tatty picture from my pocket. 'I've been looking for this boy,' I said. 'I don't suppose you've seen him, have you?'

The policeman looked at it then shook his head. 'Can't say I have.'

'He's left home,' I gabbled on. 'His mum's really worried.'

'The best thing to do is leave all the details at the station,' he told me. 'And a number to ring if he turns up there for any reason.'

'Yeah, OK, I'll do that,' I told him.

'And you're sure *you're* OK?'

'Yes, thanks,' I said. 'Honestly, I'm fine.' He didn't look as if he believed me but plodded off just the same. Wending his way down the street, past the grotty café and the clock tower, glancing up to check what it said with his own watch.

I looked at my watch too. It would be hours yet. I decided there was no time like the present. I'd go to the police now, before Mum and Dad got here.

Then I spotted someone coming towards me. Someone I knew. Roz. She didn't see me though. She put down an old blanket in a doorway outside the bookstall and sat down. She sat there, cross-legged, hassling passers-by for money.

I got up and went to her.

She squinted up at me then recognition swept over her face. 'Cass! How you doing?'

Even though my heart was hammering I swallowed nervously and said, 'Lousy.'

'Shame,' she said.

'Shame you pinched my money, you mean.'

As she stared up at me my heart stopped clamouring

in my chest. It was *her* who should feel nervous, not me.

'Don't know what you're on about,' she said, shrugging and turning away.

'Yes, you do,' I argued. I don't know how I resisted the urge to kick her. It would have been so easy and it would have made me feel so much better. 'You'd better give it back.' I knew my face was red and hot. I thought of all the things I could have done with that money. Stayed a bit longer in Dartcombe, kept hunting for James. Eat. There must be other streets, other doorways, I hadn't looked in.

But I could see it was no good. My fifty quid was long gone. I had no proof she'd taken it. No time or energy to argue.

'I still don't know what you're on about.' Roz's face had grown hard, closed up. 'You'd better shove off.'

I shrugged. She was just a waste of space. For weeks *I* was the one who'd been a waste of space. Now it was her turn. I threw a dagger at her with my eyes, turned and strolled away.

The commuters had thinned to a trickle as I made my way down the same road as the copper, dogging his footsteps towards the clock tower. I went into one of the shops to ask where the police station was.

When I got there I had to ring a bell and wait. Eventually a woman police officer came to the glass screen and slid it back.

'Yes, love, what can I do for you?'

It didn't take long to give all the details. She put them in a book and said they would be in touch if he turned up. I left the photo, taking one last look at it because I felt sure I'd never see the real James again.

Sighing, still feeling hopeless, I walked back along the High Street then down along the seafront. I felt more miserable than I'd done ever since I arrived. I don't really know what I expected. Someone to wave a magic wand and he'd suddenly turn up? I knew now that wishing simply wasn't enough.

James *wasn't* here. I might as well give up.

I saw my mother as I came back up the street towards the railway station. She was standing outside the ticket office, looking round, her eyes scanning everywhere. My dad came running round from the car park, they said something to one another then stood, side by side, holding hands, waiting.

'Hi, Mum, hi, Dad.' Stupidly I started crying as their arms went round me. I could feel them both weeping too. I was a little girl again sheltered inside them. Safe.

Why couldn't they have done this before, I thought, when I needed it so much?

'Oh, Cass!' Mum scolded, laughing, crying. 'Don't ever do this to us again.'

My dad wasn't saying anything. Just holding me, patting my back, stroking my hair.

Mum held me at arm's length. 'You look terrible.'

I laughed and cried. 'Thanks, Mum, so do you.'

'I'm not surprised,' she said. 'The last few days has put years on me.'

I gazed at her through a swim of tears. 'I'm sorry,' I said.

She shook her head. 'No, Cass,' she said. '*I'm* sorry.'

Over a hot drink at the station café I told them everything. Almost everything anyway. I left out the bit about wanting to run away for good. There was no point in hurting them any more than I'd done already. Anyway, I could see now how stupid I'd been. That old habit I was still trying to get rid of.

'We knew about James,' Dad said.

The coffee and toast had warmed my stomach and sent a glow through the whole of my body.

'How?' I wiped dripping butter from the side of my mouth.

'The school phoned, then his mother came to see us.'

'Oh,' I said. 'Poor Mrs Derwent.'

'I wish you'd told me about them,' Mum said.

I shrugged. 'What good would that have done?'

'I could have mentioned it to Janet,' Mum said. 'There are people to help women like her . . . and James. They don't have to go through all that. Doctors, the police . . . lots of people.'

'I saw Mrs Derwent at the surgery,' I said. 'Maybe she'd already told Janet?'

Mum shook her head. 'No. James's mum told me she'd made some excuse about falling over. She didn't want anyone to know what was going on.'

'Janet isn't daft,' I said. 'Surely she suspected something?'

Mum shrugged. 'Probably. But really Mrs Derwent needed to ask for help. *Then* she could do something about it.'

'Yes,' I said. 'I suppose so.'

'Anyway, she *has* asked now,' Dad said. 'So something is being done.'

'That's brilliant,' I said. 'But it's too late for James.'

I'd finished my toast and sat fiddling with my fingernails. 'I was so sure he was here.' My voice fractured. 'I can't think where else he could have gone.'

Mum patted my hand. 'Well, you did your best. Maybe he'll come back on his own?'

I looked at her and shook my head. 'No,' I said sadly. 'I don't think he ever will. Not unless someone persuades him it's the best thing he can do.'

Dad sighed. 'Well, I don't see what more you can do.'

I gazed miserably out of the window. Roz was still there looking frozen solid. I suddenly felt sorry for her. If I'd had another fifty quid I'd have given it to her. I didn't suppose she ever intended to become a thief and a druggie. Sometimes things just creep up on you and you can't do a thing about it.

'Have you had enough to eat?' Mum was asking.

'Yes, thanks.'

'OK, then,' Dad said. 'Come on, Cass.' He gave me

another hug as we got up from our seats. 'Let's go home.'

I said goodbye and good riddance to Dartcombe in my head as I got into the back seat of the car. Dad was pointing out the road signs, the one way system that meant you'd got to go all the way through the town centre to get out the other side and on to the motorway.

Mum drove down the street and turned off by the clock tower, through a maze of back roads towards the outskirts of town. I was just sitting back with a sigh when I spotted someone sitting in a doorway. They were huddled in a sleeping bag, an old tatty sports bag by their side. There was something about the dark hair, the sag of the shoulders . . .

I clutched my mum's arm. 'Mum, stop!' I was yelling, almost screaming.

'Cass, for God's sake—' she began.

'No, stop, please.'

We'd already gone past. I turned, frantically craning my neck.

Mum screeched the car to a halt. 'Cass,' she turned round. 'What on earth—?'

But I was out of the car, hurtling along the pavement, hair, jacket, flying. It was James, it was—

He looked half asleep. Face pale, hair greasy, eyes red rimmed. Ill, tired, and thinner than I'd ever seen him. He gazed up at me as I skidded to a halt in front of him.

'Cass!' A broad, puzzled grin cracked across his face. 'What the hell are you doing here?'

I crouched beside him, hardly able to stop myself crying. 'I'm looking for you, you twit.'

He struggled out of his sleeping bag. Standing beside me, he looked even worse. His clothes were filthy, his jacket torn all down the front. He smelt too, of sweat and dirt and despair.

He shook his head. 'I don't believe it. How did you know I was here?'

'You told me about Dartcombe, remember?'

He snorted. 'Yeah . . . my dream town. How could I ever forget?'

By now, my dad had reached us. Mum was sitting anxiously, the car straddling a double yellow line.

'Dad, it's James. I *knew* he'd be here.'

James didn't say anything. He just stood there, shuffling his feet and looking down at the pavement.

I took my dad to one side. 'Look, Dad, I need to talk to him. Will you give me a little while?'

Dad started to protest but then he must have seen by my face that he didn't have much choice.

'OK,' he said in a resigned voice. 'We'll find a car park and come back for you, OK?'

But I didn't want to say everything I'd got to say to James out here on the cold pavement. We needed somewhere warm to go.

'No, I'll meet you later in that café on the seafront,' I told my dad. 'The one that does all-day breakfasts. Can you lend me some money?'

My dad forked out a ten pound note and left us to it.

'Come on, James.' I took his arm. 'I'll treat you to bacon and eggs.'

The café owner was surprised to see me, coming in with James, his smelly sleeping bag tucked under my arm.

'Table for two?' he couldn't help grinning.

'Yes, please.'

I ordered food for James and sat watching him stuff it down. Then he sat back. 'Thanks, Cass, you don't know how much I needed that.'

But I did. I only had to look at him to know what a terrible time he'd had on the streets of Dartcombe.

I began telling him then. About coming to find him, Roz, the bloke in the arcade, sleeping on the beach . . . everything.

He shook his head. 'And you did it for me. Cass, you're off your trolley.'

I leaned forward, my elbows on the table. 'I had to, James. You helped me and I wanted to help you.'

He looked away, out of the window, across to the sea. 'You can't help me, Cass,' he said miserably. 'No one can.'

'But they can, James.' I told him what my mum said about the family getting help. 'So you see,' I said, 'it's OK to go back.'

He shook his head. 'No,' he said. 'I can't. I can't face it.'

I put my hand over his grimy one. 'But you've got to, James,' I insisted. 'Look, what happened to me, the abortion and everything, I reckon that's the worse thing that could ever have happened in the whole world. I wanted more than anything to run away and hide but I knew there was nowhere I could go.'

'Yeah?' James didn't look at me.

'Yes,' I said. 'And I've come through it, James. *And* I've survived a couple of nights in this dump. That's got to mean something, surely?'

He looked at me and a ghost of a grin flitted across his face. 'You had help, though,' he said. 'With the abortion, I mean. Your mum and dad . . . '

I shook my head. 'Yes, OK, they were *there*. But in the end it was something I had to face on my own, James, and I did it, didn't I?'

He shrugged. 'I suppose so.'

'And I've got over it.'

He shrugged again.

'And you'll have someone to support *you* now,' I went on.

'Yeah?' he sneered. 'Who?'

'Me,' I said.

He sat there, chewing the inside of his mouth. I could see he was having a fight with himself. I leaned forward again.

'If you don't do it for yourself,' I said, 'do it for your mum. She needs you, James . . . you need each other. You can never run away from that.'

I knew it sounded a bit like blackmail but it was true. What were families and friends for if it wasn't to stick together?

I saw his Adam's apple bob up and down as he swallowed. Then he looked at me, sighed, and shrugged again.

'Yeah,' he said. 'OK, Cass.'

Mum and Dad were waiting outside. Dad leaned back and opened the car door when they saw us come out. I went to shove the smelly sleeping bag in first. But James took it from me and stuffed it into one of the café dustbins put out for the bin lorry.

I didn't say anything.

I just grinned.

And James grinned back.

And that was how we were all the way home.